MOMMA'S A VIRGIN

ALSO BY TRAVIS HUNTER
Dark Child

MOMMA'S A VIRGIN

TRAVIS HUNTER

SBI

STREBOR BOOKS

NEW YORK LONDON TORONTO SYDNEY

Strebor Books
P.O. Box 6505
Largo, MD 20792
http://www.streborbooks.com

© 2011 by Travis Hunter

ISBN 978-1-59309-247-4
ISBN 978-1-4165-9709-4 (ebook)
LCCN 2011928045

First Strebor Books trade paperback edition September 2011

Cover design: www.mariondesigns.com
Cover photograph: © Keith Saunders/Marion Designs

10 9 8 7 6 5 4 3 2 1

Manufactured in the United States of America

For information regarding special discounts for bulk purchases,
please contact Simon & Schuster Special Sales at 1-866-506-1949
or business@simonandschuster.com

The Simon & Schuster Speakers Bureau can bring authors to your live event.
For more information or to book an event, contact the Simon & Schuster Speakers
Bureau at 1-866-248-3049 or visit our website at www.simonspeakers.com.

ACKNOWLEDGEMENTS

It amazes me that I'm writing Thank You's for my eleventh novel. I never thought I'd get past number one and if wasn't for my wonderful readers, I wouldn't have. So thanks a million. I hope you'll enjoy *Momma's A Virgin* as much as I enjoyed writing it.

I would like to thank God for all of His blessings, my son, Rashaad Hunter, for being the best kid in the entire world. Linda Hunter for you are the best mother a guy could ask for. Dr. Carolyn Rogers for always encouraging me to reach for the stars. Carrie Moses, Sharon, Christina, Aaron and Moses Capers Andrea and David, Trevor and Tyler Gilmore, BRITTANY GILMORE☺, Lynette, James (Ray Ray), Barry Moses. Amado and Amari, Hunter and Ruth Rogers, Barry Moses, Ron Gregg, Gervane Hunter, Ahmed, Ayinde, Shani, Jibade, Taylor and Sherry Johnson, my uncle Clifton Johnson, Mary and Willard Jones, Pam and Rufus, Monica (Imani) McCullough, Janera Jones, Nazarrah Rivera, Trina Broussard, Rolanda Wright, Katrina Leonce and all the Sisters Sippen tea, and all of the wonderful book clubs who read my novels. Willie and Schnell Martin, Lakecia Griffin, My agent, Sara Camilli, Charmaine and Zane. Melody Guy for getting this started and for setting the editorial bar very high from the start. To all of the wonderful people who help The Hearts of Men Foundation function. Tammy Martin, Tonietta Wheatle, Richard

Stewart, Alisa Jones, Lester Rivers III, Stefon Shilo, Jeff Cleveland, Terry Boyd, LaMont and Brandon McIntosh, Maurice Kelly, and all of the kids who keep us busy.

My industry folks, Jihad, Eric Jerome Dickey, Victoria C. Murray, Lolita Files, R.M. Johnson, Kendra Norma Bellamy, Carol Mackey, Chandra Sparks Taylor, Brian Eggeston, Nzingah, Oniwosan, Pearl Cleage, Tee Cee Royal, Tricia Thomas, Ruth Gadson, Kim and Will Roby, Kannik Sky. If I neglected to mention your name, charge it to my head, not my heart.

PROLOGUE

Zola Zaire closed her eyes and prepared for impact as the cold granite countertop rushed up and smacked her in the face. Her attacker, the man who claimed to love her, had her by the neck and was dragging her up and down the kitchen counter, knocking down dishes, glasses and canisters all along the way.

What had come over him, she wondered, as he growled like a wild animal, then lifted her up and threw her headfirst into the stainless steel refrigerator door.

"I'm so sorry, but I have to do this," Andre said. "This is gonna hurt me more than it's gonna hurt you, but it has to be done. Besides, you must've lost your damn mind. Don't you ever go snooping your ghetto nose where it doesn't belong," her fiancé snapped as he continued his assault.

Andre lifted her one-hundred-thirty-pound, five-feet-three-inch frame off the floor and over his head and slammed her down onto the hard travertine floor. Her head hit the unforgiving stone and she immediately started losing consciousness.

"If you ever try to get slick with me again," he said, "I'll beat you senseless. You'll beg me to kill you. And trust me when I say, I will oblige," Andre said with a sly smile as he pulled her back to her feet. He seemed to be enjoying the power he wielded over Zola. He held her face in his hands and looked deep into her barely open eyes.

"Aww, look at you; you can't take the pain? Well, we have to build up your tolerance level," he said as he slapped her and pulled her into the living room. "Open them eyes and tell me you love me."

Zola was vacillating between here and the afterlife. She couldn't say anything, but she realized that this had to be what dying felt like. She could feel her life leaving her body as her strength diminished. She was going to die. She knew it, because she felt her bladder release as she became weaker and weaker by the second.

Then there it was…the white light! She had heard people with near death experiences speak of a white light, but never thought that *she* would be seeing it, especially not at the age of twenty-seven. There was a tall man, skin the prettiest color of bronze she had ever seen. He had curly hair and a beard that hung well below his chest. His eyes were pleasant and inviting. The man was wearing a white robe and holding a small white dog in his arms. He smiled at her and motioned with his free hand for her to come with him. She was standing on a long dirt road, alone and naked as the day she was born, yet feeling no shame.

The man motioned again but she couldn't move. Something about him told her that she would be safe with him; she wanted to go with him, but yet she couldn't move. The man took a step toward her and extended his hand. His hands were huge, yet welcoming, but she couldn't make her feet move. She looked down to see what was stopping her and saw that her feet were buried in the ground up to her ankles. The man looked down at her feet, blew an easy breath, and her feet were free. He motioned again, but before she could move, the dog started barking and the man looked at the animal and smiled. He waved a hand at Zola, then walked away. Zola called out to him, but he and the little dog were gone and so was the white light.

She was back and Andre was still staring at her with his hands wrapped around her neck. When she opened her eyes, he released her and smiled.

"Glad to have you back," he said before throwing her face down over the back of the sofa. He ripped her dress off and removed his pants. He approached his beaten woman, rubbed his hand across her exposed buttocks, leaned over her so that his chest was on her back, and whispered in her ear, "You'd be such a good wife. It's too bad I have to kill you."

1

Ian DeMarco was sweating from every pore in his body. His mocha brown skin glistened like a crystal in the frigid air of Stone Mountain Park. He could see his destination ahead and was heading for it with everything he had. Huffing and puffing, yet he refused to stop. He had to run. Running had always cleared his mind, but it wasn't doing the trick today. He called in to work and took a personal day because he knew he wouldn't be any good. So here he was running around a big mountain with a bunch of white men carved into its side. He had already done almost five miles, and yet he still couldn't get last night's crazy episode out of his head.

His heart was threatening to beat its way out of his chest as he gripped the handles of the stroller he was pushing. The pain was kicking in. That was a good thing. Anything was a welcome relief to the images floating around his head. He had settled his mind to limit his focus to his legs and feet. He was determined to make it to the finish line and force these crazy thoughts from his head.

What was I thinking? Why didn't I just call the police?

The police? Are you kidding me? Who do you think you are? Don't you know who you are?

"Yeah, I know who I am," he heard himself say.

Ian was coming up on the point where he started running forty-five minutes ago. Five miles were in the books, and his thoughts never really left last night's drama.

Ian slowed down and walked at a brisk pace to cool down. A few minutes later he stopped altogether and reached into the back of the baby's stroller. He grabbed a bottle of water, removed the cap, and placed it to his lips. Downing the entire contents of the twelve-ounce bottle in one big gulp, he allowed two more joggers to pass, then he walked over and tossed the empty plastic bottle into the recycling bin. He turned back and went to the front of the stroller. He leaned down and smiled.

"What's up, little buddy?"

His smile was met by two sleepy eyes. "Hi, Daddy," said Christian, his four-year-old son. "I wanna get out and walk."

Ian unbuckled the seat straps and lifted his son out and onto the pavement. He watched as his son's little legs took off running.

"I'm never gonna leave you, li'l man," he said quietly. "I will not let that happen. I cannot let that happen."

"I want to play with my ball, Daddy," Christian said with a wide-eyed smile. His innocent face made his father's heart hurt even more. The little boy had no idea what he had already been through and what he had lost.

"Go ahead, but don't kick it in the lake like you did last week," Ian said.

"Okay," Christian said as he ran back to where his dad was standing, reached into the bottom of the stroller, and pulled out his basketball. He smiled at his dad, and then started dribbling the ball with his left hand. He was pretty good for a four-year-old.

Ian smiled and rubbed his son's head. He couldn't imagine life without him, yet he couldn't shake the vision of himself standing in a crowded courtroom, fitted in a striped prison outfit with two hulking guards on either side of him as the judge handed down his sentence. He could see Christian crying and reaching out for his father as the judge slammed down his gavel and ordered the guards to take him away from his son. He forced the damning thoughts from his head and tried to think of a more pleasant time. He was looking forward to the cruise that he and Christian would be taking in just two weeks. They would be leaving the cold Georgia winter for the hot sun and sands of Aruba. He could see them out on the water now, but just as quick as he smiled, the vision of him committing a crime that would ship him away came roaring back and sent bone-chilling fear down his spine; fear that would not allow him even a moment of peace.

Ian was the father of two beautiful children whom he loved very much. Brianna and Christian were his world but now only Christian was there. His beautiful wife, Tasha, and his lovely daughter, Brianna, were no longer on God's green earth, and they died because someone felt that they weren't getting their share of the almighty dollar. Money was necessary, but after losing his family because of it, Ian made a point to use as little of it as possible. His wife and daughter's lives were cut short three years ago, but to him it felt like yesterday. There wasn't a day that went by that Ian didn't relive the night that changed him forever.

Christmas had always been a special time in the DeMarco household. From as far back as Ian could remember, his father, Colin DeMarco, insisted on everybody being home and together as a family.

It was the day after Christmas, and Ian and Tasha loaded up the kids to meet his family for their annual family bowl-off. Colin was a busy businessman, but Christmastime was always reserved for his family, and he made sure to maximize his time with his kids and grandkids. This was the season that recharged him for the rest of the year. And for a man who did so much for everyone, especially his family, it was hard to deny his request to make themselves and their families available for the DeMarco

Family Bowling Night. This ritual went on every year, and it was always the day after Christmas.

The bowling alley was crowded with people who were home for the holidays. The DeMarcos had rented six lanes, and all of them were filled with family members or people who worked for the DeMarcos; people his father had always treated like family. It was a festive atmosphere, and Ian was as happy as he'd ever been. His mother, Lidia, the family matriarch, was smiling and enjoying watching her grandkids play. She chuckled when one of the small ones bowled the ball between his legs and made a strike. Ian's brother, Malcolm, and his older sister, Andrea, were arguing about something, a habit that had started when they were kids and carried over into their adult years.

"Stop cheating, Malcolm," Andrea said in her high-pitched voice. "You can't ever play fair."

"How do you cheat in bowling, Andrea?" Malcolm responded.

"You're stepping over the line; that's scratching," she said.

"Girl, I ain't that good. I can walk halfway down the lane and still miss eight out of ten. You just mad because you're losing. Again."

"If you followed the rules, I wouldn't be losing," Andrea said.

"Daddy, please tell her to shut up," Malcolm said.

Colin shook his head and rocked his three-year-old grand-daughter, Brianna, on his lap. "I'm not getting into that one," Colin said.

Ian was changing Christian's Pamper on the table in front of everybody and frowning at the smell of his son's poo poo.

"Man!" Kenny, Andrea's husband and the family comedian, yelled. "Please take that li'l rascal into the bathroom, like right now. What you got in that bottle he's sucking on, a chitterling smoothie?"

Ian laughed and continued changing his son. He looked over

at his father and he seemed like the happiest man in the world. Family had always been the most important thing in the world to him, and there was never anything he wouldn't do to make sure his people were well taken care of.

Colin DeMarco was a businessman and one of Atlanta's oldest black millionaires. He owned over twenty-seven QuickTrip gas stations as well as a part of a Texas oil field. Although his businesses brought in large sums of money yearly, they were all started with funds he had obtained in a previous life as an underworld mafia figure. That was a part of his life very few people knew about. The gas stations and oil field were all he focused on these days, but there were people in that previous life who felt cheated. Police officers, hit men, and wicked women were all used at one time or another to try and bring down the great Colin DeMarco, but they all failed and they all paid a heavy price for coming at him. Because at the end of the day, suit and ties aside, Colin DeMarco was a gangster. And he wasn't just any gangster; he was THE gangster. He had meetings with very important people—mayors, governors; he even had a picture in his office with former president George Herbert Walker Bush. To most people, Colin DeMarco was a very important man, but to some he was just a lucky nigga who got too big for his britches. Those enemies kept him on edge because he knew there were some people who wouldn't rest until he was resting in peace. Whenever Colin was out in public, he took all the necessary precautions, which explained the inconspicuous bodyguards who were peppered throughout the bowling alley.

The night was going great; balls were hitting pins; people were laughing; beer was being poured by the pitchers; and everyone seemed to be having a great time. Then a loud scream shattered the joyous occasion.

"Guuuuun!" someone screamed.

Two black teenagers with automatic weapons opened fire just behind the DeMarcos. Ian covered his son and hit the floor. He crawled toward his daughter, with Christian under one arm. He was forced to stop when a bullet hit him in his leg, burning his flesh as it pierced his calf muscle. Everything happened in less than ten seconds, but it seemed as if it took forever for the shots to stop flying. Once they did, his family would never be the same.

Colin, who was still holding little Brianna, was covered in blood and he was barely hanging on to his life, but he was the least of Ian's worries. He couldn't take his eyes off of his wife, Tasha, who was lying on her stomach with her head resting on the dirty floor, eyes open, yet motionless.

The men who worked for Colin returned fire, and the two attackers were on the floor bleeding from the many bullet holes that riddled their young bodies. Ian crawled over to his wife, but she was gone. He looked up at his father and noticed that his daughter wasn't crying. She wasn't moving either. He left the crying Christian on the floor beside his now deceased mother and jumped up and ran to his daughter. He grabbed his little girl from his father's arms and held her close to his heart. He was rocking her back and forth but couldn't bring himself to say anything.

"Brianna!" he screamed, finally finding his voice. "Brianna baby, it's Daddy. Talk to me, baby. God!" Ian screamed as he stared up at the ceiling. "Don't you do this to me! Briannnnnnnnnaa. Brianna, baby." His words were cut short by his tears. He heard his son crying and he turned and ran to him. He sat down on the floor and held Brianna in one hand and checked his son's body for blood with the other.

Andrea ran over and picked up Christian.

"I got him," she said as she cried. "Check on Brianna."

Ian turned his attention back to his daughter. He felt her neck to see if he could find a pulse, but she was already gone. It was the worst feeling in the world. He wished he could trade places with his daughter as he held her lifeless body in his arms. He sat numbly on the floor beside his wife while cradling his dead daughter.

"Call an ambulance!" somebody yelled. "Somebody please call an ambulance!"

Ian reached up and closed his wife's eyes while his filled with tears. He turned his head toward one of the teenagers who had caused all of the carnage and noticed that he was still alive. The boy was breathing hard and fighting to stay alive. Ian sat his daughter down onto a chair and jumped up. He walked over and grabbed the gun that was by the teenager's right foot. The boy looked up with pleading eyes as he opened his mouth, gasping for air. The young thug shook his head as if he was begging Ian not to finish him off. Ian wasn't the least bit swayed as he fired the final five rounds in the gun into the boy's skinny body, leaving him dead. Once the gun was empty, he reared back and threw it at the other teen who was lying upside down, already dead. The forty caliber weapon hit the boy in his face. Ian ran over to him and started beating the boy's dead body. He punched and punched and punched, but there was no amount of punishment that was going to give him back what he had lost.

Once the smoke cleared, seven people were dead and nine were wounded. Ian had lost his wife, his daughter, his mother, and the will to carry on. If it weren't for his son, he would've taken his own life.

Now, after last night's brainless moment, he was close to losing his son, too.

2

Zola opened her eyes and stared up at the water-stained ceiling. Confused, she took a deep breath as she tried to gather herself. Was she where she thought she was? This couldn't be. She had to be dreaming. She pinched herself and felt the sting. She shot up in the bed like a jack-in-the-box. Her ribs were killing her as she instinctively reached for them. They hurt even more when she touched them.

"What in the world is going on?" she said as she looked around at the seemingly familiar surroundings. Was this really real? She was hoping this was some horrible nightmare, but it wasn't.

Why was she here?

What had happened?

How did she get here?

And of all the places in the world, why here?

Zola looked around the raggedy and run-down room and felt her heart start to race. She felt as if she was about to have a panic attack. She closed her eyes and tried to calm herself by taking slow and deliberate breaths. And her head! My God, it was aching something awful. She used both hands to massage her temples hoping that would ease the pain, but lifting her arms up only hurt her ribs more.

Yet she couldn't even think about the pain, because her mind was on this space she was in. There was something about being where she was that caused her a great deal of discomfort. She tried to stop the pain between her ears by closing her eyes, but that didn't help. A tear made its way down the side of her face; she quickly wiped it away.

She couldn't cry, wouldn't cry. Her life had never allowed much room for self-pity or weakness, but now was a time she wanted to let go. *Death couldn't be this unpleasant*, she thought. The tears she tried to stop paid her no mind and continued to flow. She closed her eyes again; the stream of liquid pain kept flowing. And the fact that she couldn't stop crying made her want to cry even more.

She kept looking around the room hoping the dirty walls would magically turn into the crisp, clean walls of her own home, but the more she stared, the dirtier the walls became.

How did I get here?

She wracked her brain trying to come up with something but she couldn't. The last thing she remembered was being in her kitchen cooking dinner.

How did I get here? she thought over and over until she was mentally exhausted, yet nothing registered. Could she have been here all along, and the beautiful home that cost a few hundred thousand dollars in the trendy Little Five-Points area, had just been a dream? What about the brand-new Jaguar convertible? Was that just a dream, too? Could it all have been a fantasy? No, it couldn't be, because if it was, her life was a total failure. She had failed as a child, failed as a teenager, and now as an adult. The anxiety kicked in again and her breathing became hard and heavy.

Zola forced herself to calm down and stared at the hideous looking wall again. Her aching head got the better of her and she was forced to lie back down. Something smelled bad; she reached underneath her head and removed the disgustingly greasy and stinking pillow that had long ago lost all of its fluff. She frowned at the flat and nasty looking thing and tossed it on the floor. She wanted to cry as the realization of where she was sunk in. There were so many horrible memories in this room. She told herself that she would never enter this place again and yet here she was looking at those same pathetic walls. She wanted to jump up and snatch that ugly wallpaper off of those ugly walls and burn it, but she couldn't move. She was freezing cold and the single pane window wasn't doing much to stop the outside wind from coming into the room. The curtain flailed, letting her know that the old broken glass had never been fixed. She pulled the covers closer to her and tried not to cry.

Just yesterday she was living in heaven and now she found herself back in hell. Zola kept searching her brain for any sign of what had happened to her but kept coming up blank. After a few minutes of trying to retrace the last twenty-four hours, she stopped. She chuckled at how cruel life had been to her. It had all started in this very room. She had gone to sleep in a bed that cost almost ten thousand dollars, yet she woke up in one that reeked of urine, marijuana and sex. She was in the same bed where she was raped. The rape was supposed to be a gift for her thirteenth birthday. What in the world did she ever do to anybody to deserve what life was throwing at her?

Zola stayed on her back for a full thirty minutes saying and doing nothing. The radio alarm clock clicked to life and Mary J. Blige crooned. Zola loved Mary—well, old Mary—she couldn't relate to the new and happy Mary. But old Mary, beat up Mary, frustrated Mary, broken Mary, yeah, that was her girl. The old Mary was her kin; they shared the same spirit. The pain and anguish in every word belted from the soul sister's tortured diaphragm spoke directly to her. There wasn't a song that old Mary ever created that didn't speak of Zola's trials and tribulations in this world as a young black woman.

It was time to pull herself up and figure out what was going on in her world. And the first thing she had to figure out was how she got back in this pissy-smelling bed. And where was her evil mother? But old Mary had her paralyzed with her rhythm. The bedroom door flew open and there her mother was.

"Get yo' ass up, Zola," Sara, Zola's wicked mother, said as the door hit the wall so hard it bounced back toward her, forcing her to open it again. "This ain't no hotel. Now you let me lay down some ground rules right off the bat. Yo' ass ain't a child no more, so when I leave to go to work, you leave, too. I'mma give you today to rest up since that fool you call a man done went upside your dumb-ass head. But make no mistake about it, tomorrow you better get to moving. Yo' brother is coming home today and I promised the parole board that he had a place to stay. And he's staying in here, so don't get comfortable."

Sara gave Zola one last pathetic look as if she had smelled some sour milk, then turned on her heels and slammed the door behind her.

"Well, good morning to you, too, Mother Dear," Zola said as she sat up on the side of the bed. She ran her tongue across her lip and an instant pain shot through her body. She touched it and felt something dried and flaky on the side of her face. It had to be blood. Zola's mind raced again, trying to figure out what had happened to her, but she couldn't remember anything.

This was crazy.

She looked around and found her purse sitting on the raggedy plaid and tweed loveseat which sat in the corner of the filthy room. She grabbed her purse and looked inside for her mobile phone. Her BlackBerry screen listed seven missed calls, all from Andre. She hit the little green telephone icon and called his phone. The phone rang four times, then went to his voicemail, but she didn't leave a message. She ended the call and hit redial, but still didn't get an answer. While she was waiting for that long-winded woman Sprint hired to prompt the caller, she opened her purse and noticed that all of her money was missing. Either she had completely lost her mind, or Sara had robbed her. Perhaps it was both.

"Hey. Where are you? Give me a call. I'm at my mom's house and I…anyway, call me when you get this message."

Zola reached over toward the nightstand and turned the radio off. She sat there thinking, still racking her mind to find some answers to what had landed her back in this hellhole of a house. And what had happened to her face? She wanted to scream but what good was that going to do? She couldn't think of one single time in her twenty-eight years on this earth that she was truly happy. She stood up and felt so unstable that she almost fell back down onto the bed, but she used her hand to break the fall.

Zola shook her head to help clear it and tried again. This time she found some equilibrium and moved slowly until she felt stable enough to move quickly. She held onto the walls as she walked out of the bedroom and across the hallway into the bathroom. Once in the bathroom, she pulled the string hanging from the light switch. It was as if someone had lit a candle, but the room remained dimly lit. Zola was happy for the lack of light because what she saw staring back at her from the reflection in the broken mirror frightened her.

Oh My God!

Her face almost scared her to death. Both of her eyes were severely darkened and bloodshot; her dark chocolate-colored cheeks were now almost purple; and her lip appeared to be beyond the need of stitches.

"What in the hell has happened to me?" she said.

She couldn't believe what she was seeing. Her eyes roamed her face until she noticed the nasty gash on her forehead. It was an old scar that had somehow reopened. The original scar was given to her by a drunken Sara who would sometimes attack her for no reason. Who had reopened it was a big mystery.

Zola stared at herself. Dark skin, straight and wavy hair, high cheekbones, eyes larger than normal, yet slanted. Every time she looked in the mirror, she wondered what her true heritage was. She looked different, always had. She was always called ugly because nobody could identify with her. She was Black but mixed with something else.

Who was her daddy?

Where was he?

Did he even know she existed?

Whenever she asked Sara about her daddy, the only response she ever received was: "Why the hell you keep asking me that? Don't I take care of you good enough? Don't worry about who ya daddy is; he ain't worrying about you."

Zola turned on the water and waited for it to warm up. She placed a dab of toothpaste on the tip of her finger and brushed her teeth. The paste hurt her lip so she stopped. She bent down and rinsed her mouth out. She needed to see a doctor and wondered why she wasn't in the hospital instead of this hellhole of a house? Everything was hurting. She grabbed a hard and well-used hand towel. She ran hot water and soap over it until it was clean enough to wash her face. She looked back into the mirror and ran her hand along the scar that had been with her for most of her life.

Zola's mind went back to the day when she was nine years old and somehow had found the audacity to pour out her mother's liquor. She hated seeing that ugly green bottle of Tanqueray. Whenever that bottle was around, her mother turned into a very evil person. When Sara wasn't drinking the stuff in that green bottle, she was the perfect mother who laughed and helped her kids do their homework. She even sat at the kitchen table and played board games with Zola and all of the neighborhood kids. But once the green bottle came into place, she quickly became Satan's favorite child.

On Zola's thirteenth birthday, Sara was sipping on the contents of that green bottle pretty hard. She started drinking early in the morning and Zola couldn't help but wish her birthday was on a school day. Sara said she was celebrating her daughter becoming a woman.

"Five more years and your ass is gone," Sara said when Zola walked into the kitchen to get her morning glass of orange juice and a muffin. "But happy birthday anyway to ya ugly self."

Zola didn't speak to her mother when she was drinking so she poured herself a glass of orange juice and ignored the drunken woman.

"I know you wondering what I got you for your li'l birthday, but it's a surprise. I'll give it to you tonight," she said. "Well, *I* won't give it to you, but," Sara slurred in her drunken state, "you'll be happy. Put it that way."

Zola walked out of the kitchen and out of the house. She spent the entire day at her friend's house hoping that Zola would be asleep when she returned.

No such luck.

When Zola returned, she went straight to her bedroom and closed the door. She turned on her music to try to drown out the aggravating sound of her mother's voice.

"Happy birthday to you," Sara sang in her drunken haze. "Happy birthday to youuuu, Zola. Happy birthday to you."

Zola lay on her bed hoping that her mother would shut up, but then her bedroom door opened. She looked up to see Sara and Richard. Richard was Sara's ugly boyfriend whom nobody liked. At that moment, he wasn't wearing anything but his boxer underwear.

"Tonight is the night," Sara sang as if she was Betty Wright. "Richard makes you a woman."

Richard walked into the room and stood over her. Zola hated the sight of this man. He was black as tar and had the most rotten teeth she'd ever seen. His beard was nappy; the hair on his head was nappy; even his chest hair was nappy. It looked like some kind of burned taco meat. He started dancing a slow dance as if he was trying to turn her on. He slid his hands in his underwear and smiled. "You ready?" he asked.

"You better get your ugly self away from me! Get out of my room!" Zola yelled.

"Oh," Richard said as he moved closer to her. "Sara, we got us a fighter on our hands."

"She bet not fight," Sara said. "Get her ass tore up in here."

Zola was scared out of her mind of what the nasty man had in store for her, but she feared her mother even more. Sara's words paralyzed her.

Richard sat on the side of her bed and put his hand on her leg. She jumped and started to cry.

"Don't cry, baby girl. This gone feel good," he said. "Big Rick knows how to please a woman. And since you thirteen, that makes you a woman."

"You got to make her a woman," Sara said.

Zola protested and threatened to tell.

Sara reached back and slapped her so hard she saw stars. She didn't fight anymore. She lay on the bed and allowed the pedophile to have his way.

Zola would forever be haunted by her mother's laughter while the man forced his grown penis all the way inside of her virgin vagina.

"Ha, ha, haaaaah." Sara laughed. "Oh hush your faking. I know you been running your li'l fast ass around here with them boys."

"Noooo!" Zola cried, trying desperately to make eye contact with her mother to plead with her to put an end to this madness, but there would be no help coming.

"Listen, bitch," Sara said. "You shut all that damn whining up right now. I'm doing you a favor. You know how many girls would love for they momma to let them have sex? You ain't got a pretty bone in your body so ain't nobody gonna wanna fuck you. You should be happy you got a momma who will hook you up. Now shut your ugly ass up and enjoy your birthday present."

"Momma, please make him stop," Zola cried, but all she got was her mother fanning her off and leaving the room. She left her alone with the evil man who was on top of her, pushing and grunting as if he had lost his mind.

Zola went limp. She stopped fighting, she stopped crying, and she just lay completely still while her mother's boyfriend carried out his perverted desires with her innocent body. Once the rape was done, the man rolled over and lay on his back, trying to catch his breath.

"Aww, that was good," he said. "You okay?"

Zola was momentarily paralyzed. *What had just happened?* Her mind couldn't process it in full; she just knew that she had been violated in the worst way.

Zola calmly stood up and walked over to the raggedy loveseat in the corner of her bedroom and picked up her book bag. She unzipped the pocket where she kept her writing utensils and removed a black ball-point pen. She didn't think; she just acted.

Richard still lay in the same spot, smiling to himself. He kept that look of euphoria until Zola jumped on top of him and aimed her ink pen straight for his neck. She could feel the plastic pierce his skin and muscle.

Richard jumped up and stumbled into the wall, holding his neck while blood shot out of his wound like a faucet turned on high. He was screaming in pain but Zola was relentless. She stalked him, stabbing wherever she could reach. She punctured the skin in his back, arms, and stomach with the pointed pen, determined to return some of the pain he'd caused her. Richard's eyes bulged out as he was stabbed over and over by the little girl who had just brought him so much pleasure. Yet now he was screaming as she gave him pain like he had never experienced in his life.

A noise from the door caught Zola's attention and she realized that Sara had run into the room when she heard all of the commotion. Seeing her mother caused Zola to turn her attention and anger toward her. She stopped stabbing Richard and went after Sara with the bloody ball-point pen.

Sara screamed, turned, and ran from the house like a track star. But, Zola chased her, catching her twice in the back with the pen before Zola tripped over a tree stump and fell down. She looked up to see her mother holding her shoulder and crying for someone to call the cops.

The police showed up and Sara told the police that she had come home to find her man and her daughter having sex. She said she confronted them and Zola started stabbing the man, saying he was raping her. Then the girl flipped out and started attacking her, too. The rape had Zola in a state of shock, unable to tell her side of the story.

Zola was removed from the house and taken directly to a juvenile detention center where she was charged with attempted murder. Luckily for Zola, Richard didn't die from his multiple stab wounds and was too scared to testify on his own behalf. No one ever saw Richard after that.

Richard was gone, but Zola's memories remained and took a

heavy toll on her. That day changed everything. Before the rape, Zola was a normal kid. She got great grades and participated in any and everything her middle school had to offer. Her favorite sport was softball, and she was the starting pitcher for her school's team; but the rape with her mother's blessing, together with the lies her mother told the authorities, deadened her spirit. She became depressed and withdrawn. She rarely smiled and never played sports again.

While Zola was sitting in a juvenile detention center waiting on her day in court, she was paid a visit by her middle school math teacher, Dr. Carolyn Rogers. Dr. Rogers was a lovely woman who had an affinity for any child born into poverty. She had always had a way of getting Zola to open up to her, especially when things weren't the greatest at home.

Zola never wanted to talk about her mother's birthday gift, but as usual, Dr. Rogers figured out a way to get it out of her. Zola told her everything, and less than forty-eight hours after their conversation, the cops rushed in and arrested Sara for cruelty to children, sexual assault, and a host of other crimes. After all of the evidence was presented, it was Sara who ended up in jail instead of Zola. She took a plea deal that would sentence her to the Georgia Penitentiary for Women for nine-and-a-half years. She would get out on good behavior after only five. A warrant was also issued for Richard's arrest and he was placed on Georgia's most wanted list, but the last Zola checked, he was still on the run.

Zola was released from the juvenile detention center and allowed to go and live with her grandparents, who already had custody of Zola's younger brother, Ravon.

Momma Mary and Daddy James were already in their late seventies and not really in any condition, health-wise, to care for two energetic teenagers. Knowing they didn't have much adult supervision, Zola and Ravon ran wild. After the rape, Zola swore she would never have sex again, but somehow the exact opposite happened. She started using her body to get what she wanted from men. Money was always tight in the James's household because her grandparents were on a fixed income. The little extra they received from the state for taking custody of the two children barely fed Ravon.

Teenagers can be cruel, and if you add poverty and low self-esteem to the mix, they can be downright brutal. If there was one good thing about Sara, it was that she kept them wearing nice clothes, but that luxury went away when they went to live with Momma Mary and Daddy James. Goodwill clothes and hand-me-downs were all they would get. This transition was especially hard on Zola. She was already considered the ugly duckling, so the only redeeming quality she had was her sense of fashion. But with Sara in prison, that lone plus was now a minus.

That superficial and materialistic side led her to run around with the neighborhood hustlers. The guys who were making fast money bought her the clothes she wanted and she gave them the sex they said they needed. This simple, yet devastating, decision led her down a long and treacherous path of one bad man after another. When she turned seventeen, Zola stepped up her game. She was tired of the boys and started dating older men. She thought she had found the right man who would stop the vicious cycle, but she had a rude awakening when she realized she was pregnant. The dreams she had of them living happily ever after went flying out the window once she had the baby. She showed up at her baby daddy's office, which just happened to be the office of the ninth grade principal at her high school, and asked for assistance. She was scolded by the man, called everything except a child of God, and told to stay away from him. Once again, she confided in Dr. Rogers, the same woman who had helped put Sara away, and sure enough, the principal was brought to justice as well. But unlike Sara, the principal wasn't going to be paraded across the news as a child molester. Realizing his career was over, he placed the barrel of a .357 magnum in his mouth and ended it all right there in his office. Rumors ran rampant and Zola was forced to leave school. She never went back.

Zola rubbed the scar again as all of her past came crashing down on her. Then, all of a sudden, she looked around the small and run-down room, and realized that she had to leave. She pulled the string to turn the light off and left the room. She walked back into the bedroom where she had slept, and gathered her things. All she had was her purse, the clothes on her back, and a cashmere coat which was hanging over the arm of the loveseat. She walked back out into the living room where Sara was sitting on the same raggedy sofa they had as kids. She was smoking a cigarette and watching an episode of some reality show.

Zola stood in the doorway staring at the woman who had tried her best to ruin her life. Sara seemed old and beaten up. Her once pretty and flawless caramel skin was now filled with pock marks, dark spots, and wrinkles. Her eyes were lifeless, and her once long and silky hair was now a gray bird nest. It had been at least three, maybe four, years since Zola had last seen her mother and had she not found herself here now, forever would've been just fine. Their past would never allow them to share that sacred mother and daughter bond.

"How did I get here?" Zola asked.

Sara never looked away from her show. She laughed at something one of the actors said and acted as if Zola didn't exist.

"Well, can you tell me what happened to the money that was in my purse?"

Sara turned the volume down with the remote and turned to her daughter. "I want you to know one thing," Sara said with as much venom as she could muster. "I don't owe you nothing. I paid my price for whatever transgression you think I made against you. So, as far as I'm concerned, we are even. You rang my doorbell and I let you in. Whatever money you had in your purse when you got here should still be there," and with that, she turned back to the television and turned the volume up high.

"How did I get here? Who brought me here?"

"I don't know, Zola. I turned on the light and you were on the porch sitting in the chair. I saw a white truck, one of those SUV things, pulling off and that's all I can tell you. Now if you don't mind, I'd like to get back to my damn show."

"Why are you such a bitch? What have I ever done to you?"

"What have you ever done to me? How dare you ask me that? I went to prison because of your ass."

"You went to prison because you allowed your thirteen-year-old daughter to be raped by an old-ass man. The courts found that to be a fucking crime and so did I."

"Just leave me the hell alone," Sara said as she turned back toward the television.

"I wish it was you who I stabbed in your neck. And I wish you would've died a very slow and painful death," Zola said. "I couldn't hate you any more if I tried. You are the most despicable woman I've ever met."

"Thank you," Sara said. "Now get the hell out of my house."

Zola had to hold herself back from attacking the woman who had given her life. She looked at her mother and shook her head. She was beyond pitiful and for the first time in her life, Zola felt sorry for her. Obviously, she had some serious and deep-rooted issues that made her act this way. Zola walked over to her mother and looked down at her. The two women stared into each other's eyes, with Sara looking up from her spot on the sofa and Zola looking down on her as the child who had become the mother. Neither one of them said a word until Zola smiled, shook her head, and turned on her heels. She walked over to the door, looked back at her mother who was now sitting with her head down in shame, and walked out of the house. She had no idea where she was headed or how she was going to get there, but Zola had to leave.

3

Ian drove onto his street, which was off of Ralph David
Abernathy Boulevard in Atlanta's historic West End, and
took in his surroundings. He looked to his left and saw Harry
and Willie, two old guys whose best days were far behind them.
Life had beaten them down so much that they seemed to have
quit living. They were sitting on the curb beside each other.
Willie was a Vietnam War veteran who always wore a long
sword in a sheath connected to his belt. He was talking his raggedy mouth off while his friend Harry stared off in the distance
ignoring his drinking buddy. Willie handed a brown paper bag
to Harry and that got the attention of his hard-faced friend.
Standing behind them were a couple of younger guys wearing
big coats and looking very much the part of the low-level drug
dealers that they were. Across the street from the thugs and the
winos were a few crack addicts who were trying desperately to
sell their sickly-looking bodies to whomever could afford ten or
fifteen dollars. Ian waved at Trudy, a woman he found to be very
interesting. She was once a well-respected pediatrician who had
her own office complex in Virginia. Looking at her now, you
would think that she never finished high school.

Ian turned into the driveway of his ranch-style bungalow. His
house needed a paint job and some work done on the gutters, but
otherwise, it was in pretty good shape. He did a double take and
noticed a big, black Lincoln Town Car idling on the curb across

the street from his house. He had a visitor. His nerves kicked into overdrive.

Is this it?

Were they coming for him?

Ian took his eyes off of the car and trained them on the man standing on his porch.

"Ian," Trudy said, rushing up to the driver's side of his car. "I need a big favor. I got this little problem and… Hey, baby," she said, waving at Christian and trying to buy a little time so she could come up with a good lie.

Ian held up a hand and never took his eyes off of the man. He removed his wallet from his rear pocket and grabbed a five dollar bill. He handed the money to Trudy, but she didn't take off like she normally did. She stood there staring at the visitor just as he did.

A tall, well-dressed man stood on the porch with his hands in his pockets. He wore a suit that fit so nice it had to be custom-made. The man adjusted his black cashmere topcoat, wrapped his stylish scarf a little closer to his neck, and stepped down from the porch. A slick, black felt fedora was his crown and he tapped it in Trudy's direction.

"Hey," Trudy said, as if the man's eyes held some hypnotic potion. "How you doing?"

"Good morning; how are you?" the man said with an easy smile.

"I'd be better if I had a few dollars to get me something to eat," Trudy said, rubbing her stomach for effect.

The man smiled and reached into his breast pocket. He pulled out an eel skin wallet, opened it, and removed a fifty dollar bill. "Well, today is your lucky day. Have a meal on me."

"Thank you," Trudy said as she quickly snatched the money

from the man's well-manicured hands. "You're a very kind man. God will bless you abundantly and may all your—"

"No problem. Have a good day," he said, cutting her off in mid-sentence. There was no mistaking that his *have a good day* really meant for her to get the hell on about her business.

"You a'ight, Ian?" Trudy asked before she moved, though she was clearly twitching to be on her way.

Ian nodded his head and Trudy walked off, looking back at the man with a very suspicious eye.

Ian's fear of the authorities dissipated and was replaced by something even deeper. He was experiencing an emotion that he'd spent the last three years trying to put a finger on. To the naked eye, everything about this man said power and respect, but to him, the mere sight of him meant pain and anguish. Ian turned his vehicle off and stared at the man who looked just like him. With the exception of a few wrinkles under the eyes and on his forehead, a little salt-and-pepper hair peeking out from underneath the feathered brim, they could pass for twins.

Colin DeMarco walked toward Ian and then Colin noticed something. He stopped, shifted his course, and a wide smile appeared on his normally stoic face as he picked up his pace and headed to the passenger side of the car. He looked in the back window and almost snatched the door off its hinges to get to the smiling little boy in the back seat.

Christian stared at the man with a hint of familiarity. Then it was as if something registered, telling him that this was the man who always gave him lots of gifts.

Colin DeMarco stood in the doorway of his son's ten-year-old Ford Explorer and lifted his grandson from the seat. He gave him a quick kiss on the cheek, pushed him high into the air, then brought him back down for a tight embrace. "Oh my goodness, look how big you've gotten. Geeez, I'm going to have to stop letting so much time go by without seeing you. What's it been?" Colin said, shooting Ian a nasty look. "Six, maybe seven months. That's just shameful."

"You wanna see my car? It's my favorite," Christian said with wide brown eyes.

"Let me see what you got," Colin said.

"It's fast, too," Christian said as he twisted for his grandfather to let him down. Once he was on the ground, he jumped back into the car and retrieved his prized possession. Christian held up a yellow Corvette which had seen better days. The paint was chipped and one of the tires was missing. "I broke the tire but my dad said he's gonna fix it."

Colin reached out, grabbed his grandson's toy and studied the replica. He nodded his head. "Sporty, yet classy. I like it. Guess what Granddaddy has for you," Colin said.

"What?"

"I'll be right back," Colin continued as he walked over to the porch. "Close your eyes," he said, with his hands behind his back as he returned. "Now open them."

Colin smiled as he handed his grandson a shiny black model Lamborghini.

"Oh yeah. Wooooow," Christian said, smiling from ear to ear. He threw his tattered corvette on the ground and stood in awe of his new ride. "Thank you. Hey, Daddy, look at what Granddaddy got me. This is cool."

"That's nice," Ian said, as he walked around the truck to where his son and father were standing. He couldn't hide the fact that his feelings were a little hurt by the tossing of what used to be his son's favorite car. He walked over, picked up the old car and wiped it off.

"Only the best for my grandson," Colin said, smiling from ear to ear. He read the look on his son's face. "Relax, Ian, it's only a toy."

"So, what brings you over here?" Ian asked, cutting to the chase.

"What kind of question is that?" Colin snapped. "I have a son and a grandson standing in front of me. That's what brings me over here. Maybe if you made your way out to see me sometime, I wouldn't have to show up unannounced," Colin said. "Now act like you were raised with some sense and invite me in."

No matter how much he wanted to hate his father, Ian didn't and he couldn't. His father was a very good man to those he cared for. He was a family man to the core, but the line of work he chose had wrecked Ian's own family. And that was something he would never forget or forgive.

Ian rubbed his son's head and they walked toward his house. Once inside of Ian's small, yet tidy, home, Christian took off running over the hardwood floors to his bedroom. He returned before the two men could get into any meaningful conversation with each other. He had an armful of model cars to show his grandfather.

"Well, look what we have here," Colin said in amazement. "Man, you're a serious collector. So, which one is your favorite?"

Christian held up the new Lamborghini and then looked around for his old corvette. "Daddy, can I go outside and get my car? I must've dropped it."

"Here," Ian said, handing him the car with only three wheels.

"Hey," Christian said, reaching out for the old car. "What you doing with my car, Daddy?"

"You threw it on the ground," Ian said as he rubbed his son's bushy hair.

"So those two are your favorites, huh? I like that. Always be loyal. New stuff is cool, but old stuff has meaning. Always remember that, Christian."

"Thank you."

"Have a seat," Ian said as he fiddled nervously in the kitchen. His dad showing up was not a social call; that much he knew for sure.

Colin looked around and picked a chair facing the door. Even though Christian didn't spend much time with his grandfather, seeing him maybe three or four times a year, he acted like they were the best of friends. He jumped into the old man's lap and ran his cars on an imaginary racing track in the air. It was amazing what a new toy could do for a child.

Colin ate it up as he smiled and hugged his grandson.

"Christian," Ian said. "It's nap time, buddy."

"But I'm not sleepy. I wanna stay with Granddaddy for a little while," he protested.

"Son," Ian said in a stern voice. "What did I say?"

"Hey, big guy, listen," Colin said. "Let me see those muscles."

Christian frowned but flexed his little arm anyway.

"What the… Man, you're strong. But if you want those things to keep getting bigger, you gotta get your rest. Give me twenty push-ups," Colin said as he lifted his grandson up and placed him on the floor. "One, two, three…," Colin said, holding in his laughter at the funniest push-up's he'd ever seen. "Boy, look at him go! Sixteen, seventeen, eighteen, nineteen, twenty."

"I'm tired," Christian said, breathing hard and rubbing his arms.

"Well, give me a big hug and go do what your daddy asked you to do," Colin said as he reached out for a long embrace with his grandson. He kissed him on the forehead and savored the moment.

"Okay," Christian said.

"I know I don't get to see you that much but I want you to know that your granddaddy loves you very much, okay?"

"Okay," Christian said. "See you later, Granddaddy."

"Later, alligator," Colin said.

Once Christian was off to his room, Ian walked back into the living room. "Can I get you something to drink?"

"No, thank you," Colin said, turning to his son. His smile was now replaced by a serious glare. "I wanna know what happened last night. And I don't need you to leave out any details."

4

Zola walked down Metropolitan Boulevard toward the MARTA bus station. Cars blew their horns in hopes that she was a prostitute working the strip, but she ignored them and continued on her way. She didn't have one dollar to her name and had no idea how she was going to get back to her house, but she had to get moving. Sara's house wasn't an option. Not that she was welcome there in the first place, but even if she was, there were too many bad memories between those walls for her to even consider it. Yet there was a small part of her that wanted Sara to call out to her and ask her to come back. Maybe she could say she was sorry about everything that she ever allowed to happen and ask for forgiveness. Zola even found herself looking back toward her childhood house as she walked away, but she knew it was in vain. The woman who had given her life was physically and mentally incapable of showing any trace of motherly love.

Zola made it to the corner of Metropolitan Avenue and Eastside Avenue and sat down on the MARTA bench. The wind slapped her across her face and she felt the cuts and bruises scream in pain, but she endured. She reached into her purse and removed a large oversized pair of sunglasses and put them on. Maybe they would stop people from staring at her blackened eyes.

A bus pulled up, people got on and people got off, but she remained seated. The driver motioned with his hands as if asking her what she was going to do, but she ignored him. He closed the door and pulled off. Zola opened her purse and removed her cell phone. She dialed Andre's number again and was sent to voice-mail.

"Hey, this is me. Where are you? Call me," she said and then hit the END button on her BlackBerry.

A crazy-looking woman was standing across the street at the gas station. She wore a purple church hat, a white full-length coat, and a pair of cowboy boots. She was screaming at the top of her lungs, "All of you sinners, God has spoken to me and He has told me that Jesus is coming back soon! All sinners better repent or face the wrath! Eternal damnation is the price you'll pay!" the woman repeated over and over. "All of you sinners, God has spoken to me and told me that Jesus is coming back soon! All sinners better repent or face the wrath! Eternal damnation is the price you'll pay! All of you sinners…"

Zola stared at the woman and wondered if her chaotic message was meant for Zola. She didn't believe in coincidence. In her world, everything and everybody happened for a reason. The woman was screaming so loud that she had almost lost her voice.

Zola had not so much as picked up a Bible in her entire life. As small children, Momma Mary and Daddy James used to take her and her brother to church, but after a while, they stopped show-ing up at Sara's house to pick her up. Then, when she lived with them, they didn't even bother to wake her or Ravon up for their Sunday services. Sara was such a devil; she never even mentioned the word "church," so Zola and her brother never went, yet she couldn't block this crazy woman's voice from her head.

"You are a sinner!" the woman yelled as she pointed at Zola. Zola looked around to see who the crazy head case was talking to. She didn't see anyone else, so she turned back around and looked at the woman, who was still pointing at her. She pulled her shades down over her nose and peered at the woman.

The woman stopped screaming and leaned forward to get a clear look at Zola. Her eyes widened to the size of silver dollars and she covered her mouth as if trying to stifle a scream. She pointed to the heavens and then back at Zola.

"The devil is here!" she screamed, as if Zola was sitting on the bench with horns, hooves, and a long tail.

The woman backed up, then turned on her heels and took off running down the street with her long coat flowing behind her like a cape.

"Crazy bitch," Zola said to herself.

She sat there for a few minutes taking in the scene of people living their lives in the ghetto. She tried to block it out, but the crazy lady's words kept coming back to her. There was something there, but she couldn't put her finger on it. She wrapped her arms around herself and rocked slowly. What was she going to do? She felt alone and afraid. The last time she felt this way, she was sitting alone in a cold jail cell for attempted murder.

Zola closed her eyes, and for the first time in her life, she asked God to help her. She had never been a very religious or spiritual woman and wasn't even sure how to pray. But something deep inside of her was telling her that if there was ever a time to try this God thing, it was now. She was beaten, broken, and all alone. She closed her eyes as tight as she could and just started talking to God. She prayed as hard as she could, halfway expecting God to fix her life right then and there. When she opened her eyes, she saw an angel.

"What the hell?" Ravon, her fresh-out-of-prison brother, said with a wide smile.

Ravon stood before her showing all thirty–two of the cleanest, whitest teeth she had ever seen. He wore a pair of crisp Levi jeans, a black hooded sweatshirt underneath a big goose-down coat and a brand-new pair of Timberland work boots. A big gold chain with a medallion of the crucifixion of Christ hung from his neck.

Zola removed her shades to make sure she wasn't seeing things. "Oh my God," she said, as she jumped up to hug the one person who always had her back.

"Whatchu doing sleeping out here?"

"I'm not sleeping, boy. I was praying," Zola said as she held her brother in a long embrace. It had been five years since she had been able to touch him. She visited him about three or four times a year, and it was always behind three-inch thick prison glass.

"Praying?" Ravon said. "Now that's good to know. The last time I talked to you, I asked you to start reading your Bible, and you said thank you but you would pass."

"Did you see me reading a Bible or did you see me praying?"

"I see you still a smart ass. You look like crap. What happened to you?"

"When did you get out?" Zola asked, ignoring his question.

"Last night. Well, really about three in the morning. I'm so happy to be out of that place, I don't know what to do," Ravon said as he shook his head at the memories of a place he hoped to never see again. "It almost feels like a dream. If it is, I hope I don't wake up back in that hellhole."

"Well, try to stay out this time for more than a month or two. You've been in and out of jail since you were twelve years old, Ravon. Don't you think it's time for something different?"

"Yeah. And I promise you that I'm done with that life. Gotta leave it behind me. I'm a grown man, now. Got my girl, Lisa. She's been riding with me the whole bid," Ravon said, smiling. "That's my baby. Gonna get married and everything."

"Oh, Lord," Zola said.

"What happened to your face, Zola?" Ravon asked. His smile was replaced by a menacing snarl. "And eye?"

"I don't know," Zola said, putting her shades back on. "I need to get home."

"Whatchu mean, you don't know? That busta beat you up?"

"I don't know what happened. I woke up at Sara's house and I don't even know how I got there."

Ravon studied his sister without responding.

"So where are you headed, Zo?"

"Home."

"Where is home?"

"Little Five Points."

"Little Five Points? What you doing living over there?'

"Living, which is better than what I was doing over here," Zola said as she swept her hand around the ghetto that surrounded her and suddenly bent over in pain. "My side is killing me."

"Have you seen a doctor?"

"No."

"Well, that's where we are going," Ravon said as he walked his sister over to the gold Honda Accord parked on the corner.

"I'm alright."

"No, you are not," Ravon said.

"Whose car is this?"

"Lisa's. I'm supposed to be meeting this dude about a job."

"You're not wasting any time, huh?"

"Can't. I've wasted fourteen years of my time. In and out of that damn penitentiary. I gotta get a job," Ravon said. "I'm tired of this street crap. Going legit, Zo."

"I'll believe that when I see it," Zola said. "I wish I had a dollar for every time I've heard that one."

"Well, keep your eyes open, big sis."

"How did you know where I was?" Zola asked as she buckled her seatbelt.

"I went by Sara's, but before I could get out of the car, old nosey Ms. Ham from next door told me she saw you. She's still crazy as hell. She was standing out on the porch looking a hot damn mess. Had on a bra and a thong, trying to seduce me with those old boney-ass legs," Ravon said, shaking his head. "That chick is crazier than Sara."

"Mrs. Ham was out there? I didn't see her when I left."

"She came running out trying to hug me. The woman is nothing but skin and bones. I asked where her clothes were, and she had the audacity to tell me to come in the house with her and she'll take the rest of them off. Caked-on make-up, bright orange lipstick that missed the lips. Man, I turned around and got back in the car as fast as I could."

Zola shook her head as she pictured her old neighbor standing in the front yard in her unmentionables. Ms. Ham had always been a hot mess and would always tell anyone who would listen that she used to model for *Ebony*. She said her career was cut short because a fellow model got jealous and poured some scalding water on her, ruining her flawless face that had earned her hundreds of thousands of dollars. Ms. Ham was almost six feet tall and was so skinny you could see her bones.

"Back to Sara, I called her to let her know I was on the way, and she was ranting and raving about you and how you never appreciated her, how she was a great mom—not a good one, a great one. But I realize that Sara has some serious mental problems. You know she's crazy, right?"

"Yeah," Zola said, nodding her head. "Something is definitely wrong with her."

"I'm serious. You'd be surprised how many crazy-ass people are walking around this earth like they're regular. And all because nobody ever told them they were cuckoo."

"Speaking of crazy," Zola said. "You just missed this nut who was standing right across the street yelling at me. She kept calling me a sinner. But then, when I looked at her, she took off running down the street. I'm talking fast, too. Then she had the nerve to have on some damn cowboy boots."

Ravon jerked his head in the direction Zola was pointing. He smiled. "She scared you, hunh? That's why you're out here praying."

"She didn't scare me, but I wasn't taking any chances. I'm just saying."

Ravon laughed.

"Yeah, I hear ya. Anyway, old, freaky-ass Ms. Ham told me that she just saw you walking down the street and here you are."

"Yeah, okay," Zola said, with joy showing all over her battered face. "I'm really happy to see you, Ray."

"I'm happy to see you, too, big sis. And I know I've told you this a million times, but I'm sorry about what I did. My carelessness cost you more than I—"

"Ray," Zola said, holding up a hand to stop him from forcing her to relive a scene that took her years to get over, something she still wasn't really over. "Let's leave the past in the past."

Ravon looked at his sister and frowned. The more he looked at her, the more concern showed on his face. She had had such a rough go at life, and he couldn't bear the fact that he had added to that pain. The mere thought of what he had done ate at him on a daily basis.

"Zo," he said, "You're the strongest woman I know. Since I've been gone, I've had lots of time to reflect, and there aren't many people who could stand up to what you've been through, but I'm standing here looking at you and I'm not liking what I'm seeing. Now, the one thing I could always count on was you coming out on top, but I don't know. What's going on?"

Zola stared off into the distance. She wasn't ready for this Ravon. She could tell right away that her brother wasn't the same guy he was five years ago. He was different, wiser and more mature. But she had been down this road before, and only time would tell with him.

Her mind wandered and she couldn't help but wonder when or if she would ever find peace of mind. She could never seem to get into the groove of life because she was always fighting a new battle. But, truth be told, she had been trying to figure out why her life was always in constant turmoil. What was it about her that made life want to kick her down a long flight of stairs? Losing her son was the hardest thing she had ever endured, and she thought about him and how he was snatched away from her. Her mind drifted back to that day.

It was a Friday evening, and Zola had been looking forward to that day for two weeks. She had a hot date with a man who had something going for himself. He was a police officer, single, no kids, tall, dark-skinned, and absolutely gorgeous. To make him even more appealing, he was heavily into volunteering with under-privileged children.

Zola asked Ravon if he could come over to her apartment and babysit her three-year-old son, Jason.

Something told her to call the date off when Ravon showed up looking like he had already smoked a half tree of marijuana, but she didn't want to lose out on this good man who seemed to be crazy about her. So, against her better judgment, she made Ravon swear that he wouldn't let anything happen to her son, and headed out for a night on the town with the first man who had ever called her pretty. Everything was going better than she had planned. They were sitting at an upscale restaurant, enjoying a lovely view of ice skaters in Centennial Park. Her date talked about his dreams and aspirations as well as asked about hers. When she couldn't come up with anything, he forced her to think of something. He complimented her so much that it seemed as if he was trying too hard, yet it still seemed genuine. They finished their meals and ordered dessert. He had a hot brownie with vanilla ice cream and she had the red velvet cheesecake. Just as they were finishing up their last crumbs, her cell phone rang. She ignored it the first time, hoping Ravon was just calling to check on her. Then it rang again. She knew there was a problem, but for the first time in her life she was having a great time with a man without mentioning sex. She ignored the second call. But then, after the third call, she knew she had to get it. And something else told her that her perfect evening was about to come to a screeching halt. Oh how she wanted to hold on to just a few more minutes of bliss. But the phone seemed to ring louder with each passing second. Was it the phone or was that her mother's intuition telling her that something was wrong with her child? She looked at the man sitting across from her and knew that he was too good to be true.

"Marvin," she said. "I need to take this."

"Go ahead," he said, ever the gentleman. "Take your time."

Zola excused herself, stood, and walked to the bathroom to take the call.

Ravon's frantic scream shook her to the core. Without even being able to make out the words he was babbling through his tears, she knew something horrible had happened to her son. She ran from the restroom and rushed from the restaurant without even looking Marvin's way. Luckily, he saw her. He jumped up, reached into his wallet and dropped three fifty-dollar bills on the table before rushing after her.

"I need to get home. Something has happened to my son."

Marvin waved the valet over and told him to hurry. The car appeared in no time. He handed the young boy a five-dollar bill, and drove like a bat out of hell toward Zola's spot in the hood. When they arrived, the ambulance was already loading little Jason in the back. Zola thanked Marvin and told him she would call him later. He insisted on staying, but she wasn't hearing anything he had to say, and she jumped out of his car and into the back of the ambulance. She rode with her unconscious son to Grady Memorial Hospital.

Ravon came in and met Zola, who was now in the emergency waiting room. He sat down beside her and told her everything. He told her how they had played hide-and-go-seek, did push-ups and all of the fun things they enjoyed doing until Jason was worn out. Once the little guy fell asleep, Ravon got down to the business of bagging up his crack cocaine for resale. He took a little break from his bagging to smoke a joint and watch a few rap videos. He had been up for almost twenty-four hours straight and his body was shutting down. The weed didn't help his sleep-deprived body, because before he knew it, he was fast asleep.

At some point during the night, Jason woke up. He stumbled upon the plastic bags of crack cocaine that Ravon had carelessly left sitting on the coffee table and thinking it was candy, he took a bite. A few minutes later, the little boy started crying and trying to spit. He yelled for his uncle to wake up.

"Candy nasty," he said as his little face frowned in pain. "Candy nasty, Uncle Wayvon."

Ravon looked around and noticed that half of his drugs were tossed on the floor. He turned his attention to his nephew and jumped up. He picked him up and ran to the kitchen sink where he tried rinsing his mouth out. Jason wasn't getting any better. His crying grew louder; then he starting holding his stomach, all the while crying his lungs out. Ravon sat him down and tried to think. Jason wobbled a few times before falling down onto the apartment's floor. Ravon rushed over to his nephew who was down on all fours, gasping for air. Ravon picked him up and started patting his back but that only seemed to make it worse. He sat him on the sofa and picked up his phone and dialed 9-1-1. He told the paramedics that his nephew had gotten into some rat poison. When the ambulance arrived, the emergency tech pumped Jason's stomach, which saved his life.

Once the doctor came out and asked for Jason's parent or legal guardian, he explained that it wasn't rat poison that her son had ingested but cocaine. A few minutes later, the police showed up, followed by a state social worker.

Ravon owned up to everything and was arrested for child endangerment, but the biggest blow came when the little white social worker told Zola that they were removing Jason from her care until the investigation was complete and that she wouldn't be able to come and see him in the hospital until a decision had been made. She was only eighteen years old. She had been living on her own in the projects with a plan to get her and Jason a better life, but once she realized she was losing her son, she all but gave up on living.

Zola looked at Ravon as he drove. She had already gone through every emotion possible when it came to him. She wanted to hate him, but she couldn't.

Ravon seemed to be deep in thought. She reached over and rubbed his leg.

"It's okay, Ray."

"How is it okay?"

"It just is," she said as she reached in her purse and pulled out her phone again. She hit a few numbers, dialed Andre, and got his voicemail again. "This idiot isn't answering his phone and I don't even have enough money to catch a bus home."

"When I talked to Sara, she said that your dude beats you," Ravon said slowly, with a dangerous undertone. "You mind talking about that?"

"How would she know?"

"Looking at your face, I would say she might be onto something, Zo," Ravon said.

"I honestly don't know what happened. He has never hit me before, but I'm drawing a blank on this and I don't know why. It's driving me crazy."

"You don't know, huh?" Ravon said, shaking his head. "I don't understand you women. You stay with guys who beat you and then make excuses for them or try to protect them."

"I'm not making an excuse. I don't remember what happened. Turn here," she said, pointing toward the I-20 East marker.

"I'm taking you to the hospital."

"We can go to the hospital later, but I need to go home first," Zola said as she pulled down the passenger side sun visor and looked at her face. "Oh, my goodness."

"Zo," Ravon said, shaking his head. "You need to see a doctor. Like right now."

"I know, but take me home first."

5

I an walked into the living room where his father was sitting
and took a seat on the sofa across from him. He took a sip of
his coffee and set the mug down on the end table beside him.
He rubbed his hands together and took a deep, thought-gather-
ing breath. He blew the air from his lungs and shook his head.

Colin didn't say a word.

Ian stared at his father. He realized that he missed their relationship. They were always close, but every time Ian saw him, he
couldn't help but think of all the pain he suffered from losing his
family.

"I was coming home from work," Ian started, but stopped again.
He couldn't believe what he had done. Somehow his life just didn't
pan out the way he had expected.

Colin didn't push his son. He sat back in his chair and crossed
his legs as if they were having a leisurely Sunday chat.

Ian looked through the bars of his living room window at the
people passing by outside. He was trying to find the right words
to explain his actions.

"I don't like living over here anymore," he said. "I thought I
would like it. Thought I could make a difference around here,
but these people don't want to change. They've been living like
this so long they don't know how to change."

Colin didn't respond.

"If I'm going to hell, then I might as well experience a little heaven while I'm here on earth. That is, if I don't end up in prison."

Colin still didn't say anything.

"Do you know this house has been broken into ten times since we moved in here two years ago? Ten times, Dad. And on top of that, they did it while I was at work. I'm working and they're stealing."

"Son," Colin said, motioning with his hands for Ian to tell him what he came to hear.

"Yes, sir," Ian said. "I was thinking out loud. That's all."

"Tell me what happened last night," Colin said, cutting to the chase. "I have somewhere to be."

"I'm gonna tell you," Ian snapped. "Will you give me a minute? I'm trying to tell you what's been bothering me. Do you mind? Can I at least have a decent conversation with my father before I get into any of this other crap?"

"Sure," Colin said. "I apologize. What's on your mind, son?"

Ian sighed again. He was stressed and it showed in the wrinkles in his forehead.

"I was thinking about moving. I don't want my son growing up looking out of bars that are over his bedroom window."

"Well, move. You can live anywhere you want, Ian. You know that. You were born into wealth. This was your choice to live here. It was your choice to turn away from your family. It was your choice not to use your Master's degree and instead to go work with guys with GED's on a garbage truck. Maybe you figure that's your way of punishing me?"

"No," Ian said with a frown. "Why does everything have to be about you?"

"I'm only asking a question, son."

"Well, no. I don't know what it's about."

"Okay. You're grown and I'm sure you'll figure it out," Colin said. "I'm always here for you. You're my son and you'll always be my son."

Ian looked at his father. He was a stern man. A hard man who had lived a hard life and he made no apologies about how he earned his living. It seemed the only soft spots in his heart were reserved for women and children.

"It was raining hard last night. I could barely see," Ian started as his mind flashed back to last night.

Ian had just pulled his trash truck into the parking lot; he did his final checks and shut it down. He jumped out and ran into the City of Atlanta Sanitation Department office and turned in his keys. He punched his time card and slipped it back into his slot.

"Y'all have a good evening," he said to the secretary. He never knew nor asked her name. "I'll see ya in the morning."

"Bye, Ian," she said as she did a quick flick of her tongue and flirted with her eyes.

"I'm sexually harassed every day up in here. I'm filing charges on you tomorrow," he said with a smile.

"Oh, you're wrong for that. But listen," she said seductively. "If I'm going to get fired, then I think we should sneak off into one of these offices and make it worth my while," she said.

Ian shook his head and fanned her off. He threw his jacket up over his head and ran from the building. He ran hard to avoid the pouring rain and jumped into his Ford Explorer. He turned the ignition and it wouldn't catch.

"Come on, man. Not today," he said as he popped the hood and got out of the vehicle. He didn't even bother to cover himself from the rain as he looked under the hood.

"You need some help, brodda?" Walker, one of his co-workers, asked.

"Yeah," Ian said. "I think I need a jump."

"You got battery cables?"

"Yeah," Ian said.

"Me gone pull round," Walker said, and pulled his car around so that his was facing Ian's. They hooked up the jumper cables to the cars' batteries. Ian jumped back in and turned his ignition. After a few stalls, it started.

"Thanks, man," Ian said as he jumped out and shook Walker's hand. "I owe you one, my friend."

"No mention it," Walker said, shaking his head. "It's no big deal. I like to help. Hey, Ian, you got a second?"

"Yeah," Ian said as he ran around Walker's car and got in the passenger side.

"It's 'bout to start getting colder out chere. You might wanna look into replacing dat old battry, brodda."

"Yeah, I'mma run by Pep Boys on the way home. What's on your mind, big man?"

Walker sighed and shook his black face. He seemed to be hurting inside. He looked down at his long fingers and rubbed his wedding ring.

Walker's real name was Dabab Lulubo Abdullah. He was born and raised in the Sudan and spoke with a heavy African accent. He was also almost seven feet tall and walked with a pronounced limp, an injury he'd suffered fighting in the Sudanese war when he was a child. Walker fled to America when he was eighteen years old, with the help of American aid workers, to avoid the bloodshed that had plagued his homeland for as long as he could remember. Walker took a liking to Ian because the quiet man never made fun of him like the others and seemed to be an intelligent man. The others only seemed to be into having fun and laughing their lives away, so Walker stayed clear of them and latched on to Ian.

"I need to get on out of here, but I need some advice from you, brodda."

"What's up?" Ian said.

"My wife may be cheating on me."

"What makes you think she's cheating on you, Walker?"

"She doesn't wanna to have intercourse no more. Been two weeks. Two loooong weeks, brodder, and I'm 'bout to die. I didn't get married to sleep alone."

"So because she doesn't want sex, you think she's cheating?"

"Yes," Walker said emphatically.

"Is she hanging out late, getting phone calls, text messages from men?"

"No," Walker said, shaking his head. "But women sneaky creatures, brodda. We can't outsmart dem. No way in hell."

Ian chuckled.

"So because she stopped wanting sex, you think she's cheating?"

"Women need it, too, brodda, and if she's not getting it from me, den what am I supposed to tink?" Walker asked, frowning so much that his bald head wrinkled.

"Walker, y'all have four kids. And you are only what? Twenty-six? How old is she?"

"Twenty-four."

"The woman might be tired," Ian said with a smile.

"You tink so?"

"Perhaps. Is that the only reason you think that she's cheating?"

"Yeah," Walker said. "I need good loving every night, man."

Ian smiled. "That good loving every night may not be so good to your wife. Stop being selfish."

"Okay," Walker said, nodding his head. "You know deese American women; I don't. In my country, a woman doesn't have de option to tell her husband 'no' in de bedroom. Dat's grounds for an ass whipping."

"Well, you are in America now and women are very different. Especially black women. Trust me! You will get your own ass whipped."

"Negative."

"Okay."

"Man, she got me taking college classes at night over at de college. Said I can't be a trash man my whole life, but I make more money dan her. She's a teacher wit' two diplomas from universities."

"If that's all you have to worry about, then I don't think she's cheating," Ian said, smiling at his friend.

"You tink? Good. But hey, she lazy, too, man. Don't wanna work both shifts with de children. You know we got dem twins and dey just turned two. Terrible twos, brodda, and I mean dey terrible, ya hear me? Tear up every damn ting in the house," Walker said, smiling from ear to ear. "I swear, Ian, they'll tear up a nail if given de opportunity."

Ian laughed and shook his head. He could tell his friend loved every minute of his family.

"I like being married, Ian. I really do. But my wife is the pits. You are one lucky man. To be single," Walker said, savoring in his mind the freedom he once had.

Ian's smile faded. He'd give anything to have his wife back in his life, but none of his co-workers knew much about his past. "Well, Walker, I need to run. Besides, we need to get out of this rain. Take care of them babies and give your wife a break. It's tough handling two two-year-olds along with two other kids. And you guys have all boys?"

"Yeah," Walker said. "Strong sperm run in my tribe, brodda. I'll see you tomorrow, my friend."

Ian got out of Walker's car and got back into his truck. He pulled out of the parking lot and onto the access road. He drove slowly because he couldn't see very far in front of him. He made his way to I-285 and merged onto I-20. He got off on Moreland Avenue, made a right off of the exit and headed to Pep Boys, where he purchased a battery and some air fresheners. He walked back outside and removed the old battery and installed the new one right there in the parking lot. He jumped back into his SUV and was happy when it started up without a fuss. He eased out of the parking lot and turned back onto Moreland, heading back to I-20. Just as he turned the radio up, out of nowhere, a woman ran out into the street and stopped right in front of his truck. He slammed on the brakes so he wouldn't run her over. Once his vehicle stopped, he slammed his gear shift into park and jumped out to see what was going on. The woman had dropped to her knees right there in the middle of the street.

"Are you okay?" he asked.

"Help me," she said in a weak voice.

People blew their car horns at Ian and some gave him the finger as they rode by. He ignored them and leaned down to help the woman to her feet. She seemed to be pretty young, maybe twenty-five, but no older than thirty years old. She was bleeding from her mouth and the area around her eyes was puffy and discolored.

"Can you stand?" Ian asked.

"Yes," the woman said, looking around dazed and confused. Was she high? He wondered.

All of a sudden, the woman let out an ear-piercing scream and used what little strength she had to clutch his arm. Ian turned his head to see what she was so afraid of and what he saw even startled him. A tall and well-built man came at the woman with the aggression of a lion stalking his prey.

"Mind your fucking business, potna. This is my bitch. Bought and paid for," the big man said as he reached out and grabbed the woman as if she were an unruly child. "Get yo' ass back in that damn house. What the hell is your problem? Have you lost your damn mind? Running out in the street like some stray cat."

Ian felt the woman trying to place something into his hand as the big man was pulling at her.

A set of keys.

Ian took them and eased them into his pocket before the big man could see what had happened. The man grabbed a handful of her hair and dragged her out of the street, barely missing being hit by a passing car. The big man stopped and held up a fist to the passing driver as he stepped up on the sidewalk. He turned around and gave Ian one last warning look.

Ian stared at the couple. The woman didn't take her eyes off of him. She was pleading with her swollen eyes for him to help, but he just stood there. He had to do something, but what? Nothing irked him more than a coward, and a man who would hit a woman, under any circumstance, was a true coward in his book. Yet, standing there in the rain doing nothing, it was he who felt like the coward.

Ian knew right then and there that he wasn't going to leave that woman alone. He couldn't get in his truck and go on about his business, knowing that there was someone out there who he could've helped. And since God set his day up so that he would be right here and right now, she *was* his business.

Ian stood there in the pouring rain, unable to take his eyes off of the poor woman who was doing everything except begging him to help her.

"Hey man!" he yelled. "Leave that woman alone."

"Or what? What you gonna do about it?" The man growled, swung a big silver pistol up and pointed it at Ian. "Come on and play Captain Save a Hoe and I'll drop you where you stand."

"Big tough guy with a gun. Put it down and deal with me like a man," Ian said.

"You better get on 'bout ya business, potna," the big coward said as he turned away.

"Put the gun down. You're tough. Tough enough to beat a woman. Come try that with me," Ian said, trying to keep the man from taking the woman out of his sight, but to no avail. The coward ignored him and dragged the woman into the parking garage.

Ian couldn't believe what he was witnessing at seven o'clock in the evening. The streets were still filled with people, yet nobody said or did anything. The people hurried by or kept driving as if they couldn't see what was happening. The poor woman was alone in a city full of people. He took a deep breath, walked back to his truck and got in. He didn't move. He found his cell phone and dialed 9-1, but couldn't bring himself to dial the other "1." People stood on their horns, urging him to move out of their way, but he just sat there.

"Oh, give it a break. Woman is out here getting her brains beat out and y'all in a rush to go do what?" he said to no one in particular.

He looked in his rearview mirror and an old white man stood behind him, blaring his horn non-stop. He got out of his truck and walked toward the man. He stopped at his door but the man wouldn't look at him. He knocked on the window but the man kept looking straight ahead, still sitting on his horn. Ian snatched open the man's door.

"Stop blowing your damn horn or I will snatch your old ass out of this car and beat the shit out of you."

The old man slammed his car in reverse, not caring if he hit anyone or not. He hit his brakes, put his car back in drive, and sped around Ian's truck.

"You should've done that the first time, asshole," Ian said, walking back to his vehicle. His thoughts went back to the woman. He looked at the building that the man had dragged the woman toward and counted the floors. It was a four-story building; three were used for living space, and the bottom level was the garage. He put on his signal light and turned into the garage. He pulled into a parking space, put his truck in park, and pulled out his cell phone. He called his baby-sitter and told her that he would be a little late and that he would take care of the extra cost once he arrived. Once he hung up, he sat there. Waiting. He wasn't sure what he was waiting on, but he realized he had jumped into this mess headfirst. He reached into his glove compartment and removed his gun. He hated guns but knew that in this crazy world sometimes you had to fight fire with fire. Ian stepped out of the truck and slipped the gun in the small of his back, beneath his belt.

Ian got out of his truck and surveyed his surroundings. He listened for sounds of the battered woman as he slowly walked toward the door leading into the building. There was an elevator right beside the glass doors. He decided to take the elevator. He pushed floor number two and waited. The doors opened, and he stepped off and walked down the hallway. He stopped and placed his ear against the first door, only staying a few seconds so he didn't look too suspicious. He moved on to the next door and did the same thing. He walked the entire hallway doing that, yet didn't hear anything out of the ordinary. A few television sets, kids crying, some loud music. He even heard a couple making love, but nothing out of the ordinary. After checking every door, he made his way to the staircase and walked up to the next floor. He started the same routine of listening at the doors. He didn't hear anything out of the ordinary on this floor either, so he hit the stairwell again. He was on the top floor and repeated his ritual as he walked down the hall. After checking four doors, he heard what he was there for. The big man's voice boomed, but he didn't hear the woman. He stood outside of the door listening with his ear to the door. A young, white girl with long blonde hair was walking down the hallway toward him. She had on headphones and seemed to be in her own world.

Ian fiddled around with the key the woman had given him and acted as if he was looking for his cell phone. The white girl stopped and opened the door next to the one he was standing in front of. He slid the key into the lock and before he opened the door, he snuck a peek back at the white girl and she looked right into his eyes. He couldn't turn back now; he opened the door and walked in. The man from the street was standing with his back to him and obviously didn't hear him enter his domain. The big man had on the same blue shirt he had on outside, but his pants were down by his ankles as he yelled obscenities at the woman while his hips gyrated back and forth. There was no doubt he was having sex with her, but the woman didn't make a sound.

Ian walked up behind the man who was wrapped up in his deviant sexual act. Ian was close enough to touch him. He removed his pistol and placed it at the back of the man's head.

"I'm the man," the big man said as he had sex with the woman. "And you need to learn how to stay in your place. You gonna run out on me? I'll teach you."

Fifteen years of karate lessons were all coming down to this. Ian slid his gun back where he had it and tapped the man on his shoulder. Startled, the man let out a girlish scream and jumped. When he turned around, his eyes registered instant fear. Ian took his right hand and, with all of his force, punched the man with the heel of his palm. The blow hit the big man under the nose and forced it up, causing a hideous cracking sound. The man opened his mouth but nothing came out. Ian struck him in his neck and the man's hands flailed as he tried to break his own fall.

Ian never made a sound as he pounced on the man. He kicked him in his groin and the man gave up. His eyes were wet with moisture as he lay there on the cold stone floor of a high-priced condominium, half-naked, and beaten half to death. The man's eyes rolled into the back of his head as if he was begging for the angel of death to come take him away from the obvious pain he was in.

Ian looked at the woman; she was still bent over the sofa with her rear end exposed. He tried to lift her, but she was dead weight. He looked back at the big man who was trying to pull his pants up as if he wanted to die with a little dignity.

Ian stood still. He couldn't move. No one was moving. The woman was still laying over the edge of the sofa as if she was asleep. The big man was on the floor, staring up with dead eyes.

Ian shook the woman. She wasn't moving. He checked her pulse and found one. He pulled up her pants and lifted her up. He looked around and saw her purse and coat sitting on the chair. He hurried over and grabbed the purse and the coat. He lifted the woman up as if she were a baby and hurried out of the condo. He walked down the hallway to the stairwell and quickly made it back to the garage.

He shook the woman to try to wake her, but she was in bad shape. He thought about driving her to a hospital and dropping her off but thought that was a bad idea. He went through her purse and found a driver's license. He searched the address and realized it wasn't the one where they had just left. He punched the address in his navigation system and followed the instructions until he was at a house in the hood.

IAN WRAPPED UP HIS STORY AND TURNED TO HIS FATHER WHO was still sitting with his legs crossed and his hands on his knees, just as cool as ever.

"I see," Colin said.

"Now what?" Ian asked.

"You should use your head a little more before you act next time."

"I did use my head. Thanks to you, I don't feel comfortable calling the police."

"There you go, Ian. Blame your troubles on anybody but the man in the mirror. You can call the police like anybody else, but you would rather soak in your misery. I lost as much as you lost in that bowling alley, but life goes on. I hate to sound cold, but you're going to have to snap out of this depression, son. You have a son to raise, but you have him living over here in squalor because you're mad at me. Well, that's smart. "

"I'm not mad at you, Dad," Ian said as a tear made its way down his cheek. "I can't get over the fact that my family is gone."

"Your family is not gone. You have a beautiful son, a sister, a brother and I'm still here. Are things perfect? No, but they're better than you're allowing them to be."

Ian nodded his head while looking at the hardwood floor. "How did you know about last night?"

Colin didn't answer. He stood, took a deep breath and walked over to peek in on his grandson.

"Always think of him first," Colin said, turning around to face his son. "You did a very dangerous, not to mention stupid, thing, Ian. That wasn't your business."

"So, what now?" Ian asked, wringing his hands together just as he did when he was a child and found himself in a situation where he needed his father to fix his mess.

"Now," Colin said. "I'll take care of it. Go on about your business, as if this whole incident never happened."

"But I killed a man," Ian said.

Colin gave him a side-eyed look, reminding him that this wasn't his first kill and that he had taken care of it then and he would do the same this time.

"Your sister is cooking dinner on Friday. I expect you to be there. It's time you come out of your hole and rejoin the world."

6

Zola was lost in a daze. She really needed to see a doctor, but something was pulling her to go home. She needed to get a grip on things as soon as possible or risk going completely crazy. She told Ravon to get off on the Moreland Avenue exit and to keep straight. They got caught at a red light and as they waited for the light to change at Memorial Drive, Zola noticed something. She was looking at a man who was pumping gas into a black pick-up truck. There was something about the man that held her attention. She scanned him up and down. He was wearing a green work shirt with matching pants, black work boots and had a pair of white work goggles perched on his head. She wondered why he wasn't wearing a coat. Her eyes burned into the man's face, but he didn't look familiar. So why was she staring at him so hard? There was something about this man that was calling her name.

The light changed and she was tempted to ask her brother to pull into the station but she decided not to. They drove along Moreland, passing through an area that was in the midst of gentrification. The poor residents were being forced out by the dozens and being replaced by the buppie crowd. On one corner, they passed a dilapidated house and on the next, a high-price condominium was being built.

"Stop," she said, as she remembered something that might lead her to one of the answers to the many questions bouncing around her head. "Pull over right here."

"Zo, I can't pull over in the middle of the street," Ravon said, looking in his rearview mirror for clearance.

"Just stop," Zola said as she pulled at the door handle.

"Wait a second," Ravon said as he maneuvered the Honda out of the street and into the parking lot of Chase Manhattan Bank.

Zola got out of the car and walked over toward the sidewalk. She stopped and stood there. Something about this spot was calling her name. What was it? She remembered being in the street and screaming but she couldn't put the rest of the pieces of the puzzle together.

Ravon got out of the car and walked over to her. "You okay, Zo?"

"I'm not sure what I am, Ray," she said, confused and pointing at the busy avenue. "I was out in this street. I think I got hit by a car, but I can't remember what the hell happened."

"Hit by a car?" Ravon asked with a frown. "What makes you think you got hit by a car, Zo?"

"I remember lying down in that street. That much I do remember," she said, scratching her head, trying to force the memories back. "But what was I doing in the street?"

"And you think whoever hit you was the one who took you over to Sara's?"

Zola shook her head. "I don't know, but I was in that street. This is as weird as it comes, man. I'm not crazy, but I can't remember anything."

"Are you okay?" Ravon asked as he placed a hand on his sister's shoulder.

"No," Zola said, looking around and taking a deep breath. "I'm not okay, Ray. But I do know that something happened to me right here."

Ravon walked her back over to the car and helped her into her seat. He walked back around, jumped in the driver seat and turned to his sister.

"Zo," Ravon said, "I'm here for you. You don't have to fight this thing alone. If there is anything I can do for you, let me know."

"Thanks," Zola said, but her mind was still racing.

They pulled out of the bank's parking lot and back onto Moreland. Then, less than one hundred yards from the bank, Zola told him to turn into an underground garage. They parked and got out of the car. Zola placed her purse on the hood of the car while she searched for her keys. She dug all around the big Coach duffle bag but couldn't find them.

"Okay," she said, frustrated. "Now where are my keys?"

Ravon stood staring at his sister. not knowing what to think. He hated every misdeed that was ever leveled against her. His heart ached for her and he made a vow to do whatever he had to do to lighten her load.

"I need to run into the front office and get a key. Come on."

They walked through the glass double doors and into the eclectic lobby of the Select Condominiums. The builders spared no expense when constructing the living quarters. Marble and glass were everywhere, from the floors to the ceiling. One of the largest leather sofas known to man sat facing an equally large fireplace. On the opposite wall was a huge fish aquarium that faced the street, so anyone passing by could see sharks and a small dolphin, as well as blue, yellow, green, and orange fish. The aquarium was filled with all kinds of weird, yet exotic-looking aquatic wild life.

"Hi there, Zola. How are you doing today?" Kecia, the receptionist, said as her face registered the shock she felt when she took in Zola's swollen face. Kecia White was in her early twenties and was pretty as a baby. Her deep chocolate skin was flawless. She had large, sleepy eyes that reminded Zola of a doe. She kept her hair in a short natural and had it faded on the sides. Kecia worked at the condo as a means to help pay her own way through law school. She was as on the ball as anyone Zola had ever met. Her easy smile and comforting demeanor never let on about her rough-and-tumble past. If you didn't know any better, you would think Kecia was born with a silver spoon in her mouth, but she came up on the hard streets of Brooklyn. She had no recollection of her prostitute mother, because she was killed by one of her johns before Kecia's first birthday. Her father was an unknown, which meant he was probably one of the many men who roamed Brooklyn's streets searching for a cheap thrill between the legs of women who had lost all hope of ever being anything in life. Kecia was raised by her mother's pimp and his stable of raggedy-looking prostitutes. The women took care of Kecia's basic necessities such as food, clothes, and shelter, but that was about it. Knowing the legal age of consent in the state of New York was seventeen, she made sure to take summer school classes so she could graduate from high school by her seventeenth birthday. She didn't want there to be any chance of her mother's pimp suggesting that she become a part of the street life. On the day of her high school graduation, she packed her bags, walked to the Greyhound bus station and purchased a ticket to Atlanta. Once the bus made it to the station, she caught a cab to Spelman College and met a blessing. As luck or fate would have it, she bumped into one of her favorite authors, Pearl Cleage. Kecia shared her story with Pearl and the author/lecturer worked her magic. Not only did Pearl get Kecia accepted into Spelman, she took care of her living situation while she was in school by inviting her to live with her and her husband Zaron until she could secure housing on campus.

With Pearl's help and mentorship, Kecia graduated near the top of her class after three years and jumped right into the law school program at Emory University.

"Hi, Kecia," Zola said. "I've been better, but how are you?"

Kecia kept her professional demeanor, but her eyes betrayed her. One thing that Zola had found out about Kecia in their many talks was that the girl knew how to mind her own business. No matter how many times she tried to get some gossip started with Kecia, the girl never fed into it.

"I lost my key," Zola said as if this was just another day. "Don't ask me how, but it's gone."

Kecia nodded her head and pulled out a log. "No problem. Just sign right here and I'll run and grab you the spare. Now, you know it needs to be returned within twenty-four hours, right?"

"Now I do," Zola said with a slight smile that still hurt her lip.

"Cool. Just letting you know because they charge like two hundred dollars or something like that if it isn't returned. I'll be right back," Kecia said as she stood and walked behind a wall.

"Damn, Zo," Ravon said. "Now I hate to be selfish because I know you wanna get to your place and lay down, but that chick is off the chain. Make the introduction?"

"Awww," Zola said, scratching her temple as if she was really thinking about it. "No."

"Why?"

"Because she's about her business and she's out of your league. Plus you have a woman. Stop being a typical man."

"What's my league?"

"Hood rats."

"That's not true. I'm a changed man, Zo," Ravon said. "And how you gonna call my girl a hood rat?"

"Hush, Ravon."

Ravon fanned her off and walked over to the wall-length salt-water aquarium. He was completely amazed at the size of the tank. "Look at this thing, Zo. I know this cost at least twenty-five grand. I wonder if I can steal it."

Zola shook her head. "Changed man, huh?"

"I'm just saying. Y'all got a mini Georgia Aquarium up in this joint."

"Yeah," Zola said, nodding her head. "It's very relaxing. Sometimes I come down here at night to read and watch the fish swim around. Their only worry is when they will eat."

"Hell, that's most people's worry, too," Ravon said. "But not y'all. This is what you call living. Damn, I gotta get my act together."

"Since you're changed now, I'm sure you'll be back on track in no time," Zola said. "My head is killing me."

"I can still take you to the hospital," Ravon said as he ran his finger across the soft leather of the sofa. "Damn, sis, you done came up."

"Not really." Zola sighed.

Kecia came back with the key and Zola signed for it.

"Thanks, and I'll be sure to get this back to you before my time expires," Zola said.

"No problem," Kecia said, handing Zola the key. Before she released it, she said, "I'm taking a few days off and then I come back and...well. I hope you'll call me if you need anything."

"How are you doing today?" Ravon said, interrupting the sisterly moment. "I'm Zola's brother."

"How are you, Zola's brother?" Kecia asked, as her eyes lingered on Zola.

"My name is Ravon," he said as he waved his hand to get her attention. "I'm over here."

"Nice to meet you, Ravon," Kecia said, slowly turning to face him.

Ravon reached out his hand to her and was met with a firm handshake in return.

"Maybe we can exchange numbers or something," Ravon said. "You are probably one of the sexiest women I've ever seen."

"Thank you for the compliment, but I'm going to have to pass on the number exchange," Kecia said as she took her seat and turned her attention back to her computer. "Anyway, I need to get back to work."

"Oh, it's like that?" Ravon said with a frown.

"Like what?"

"You're blowing me off. I guess I don't have the look for your type, huh?"

Kecia gave him a condescending smile as if he was a little boy with a crush on his grade school teacher.

"Wow," Ravon said. "Black women."

"Black women?" Kecia said, looking up. "What's wrong with black women?"

"Y'all attitudes suck. Here I am trying to be respectful," he said, "and all you can do is ignore me."

"And I was respectful to you. I'm just not interested."

"Why?" Ravon asked.

"Because I don't have to be," Kecia said.

"I guess I'm not your type, huh?"

"Nobody's my type right now, Ravon. I'm in school and I don't need any distractions. Is that okay with you?"

"Nope," Ravon said with a frown. "I wanna take you out. Prove to my parole officer that I'm running with a different crowd."

"Oh, Lord," Kecia said, laughing. She looked at Zola for some help.

"Come on, boy," Zola said, shaking her head. She grabbed Ravon by his arm and led him to the elevator.

"Have a good day, guys," Kecia said and turned back to her work.

Zola and Ravon got on the elevator and Zola hit the button with the Roman numeral IV on it. There was a slight jerk as the elevator carried them up to the fourth floor. Just as they stepped out of the elevator, they saw a police officer walking toward them.

The officer, a short and stocky white guy with a buzz haircut stopped right in front of Zola's door and waited for them.

"May I help you?" Zola asked.

The officer inspected Zola's condition and frowned. "Ma'am, do you live in this building?"

"Yes, I do," Zola said.

"Were you here last night, let's say...around eleven o'clock?"

"No, I wasn't," she said. "You're standing in front of my door."

"Mind if I ask where you were?" he asked with a skeptical look on his face.

"Why?"

"There was a robbery that took place last night next door to you and I was wondering if you saw anything," he said.

"No," Zola said. "Like I said, I wasn't here."

The officer gave Ravon a once-over from head to toe, then nodded his head. "May I ask what happened to your face?"

"I fell down," she said.

"I see," he said, reading her lie. "Ya'll have a good day."

Zola placed the key in the lock and turned the knob. Once inside, she paused. It was as if the beating was coming back to her. She could see Andre dragging her around the condo by her hair. She shook the visual from her head and walked into the kitchen. The place was spotless, yet she remembered the kitchen being tossed around pretty good. Plates and canisters were all on the floor. She specifically remembered the ceramic cookie jar breaking on the floor as she was being dragged down the counter. She walked over to where she kept it and the jar was gone. She opened up the pantry door and looked in the trash can, but there was a fresh bag in there.

Zola stopped and scratched her head. Then she ran to the guest room closet. She flung open the door but there was nothing inside. That was where Andre had kept his clothes and now there was no sign of him.

"The key," Zola said, turning to her brother.

"What key?" Ravon said perplexed.

"I gave my key to this man I met on the street. He stopped to help me and I gave him my key. Oh, my God."

Ravon frowned. "Stopped to help you? Who stopped to help you? And what was he helping you do?"

"This man," she said. "I remember running and Andre was chasing me. Then this man stopped his truck and I gave him my key."

She walked around the two-bedroom condo looking for signs of anything that would help jar her memory. "I wonder where he is," she said.

"Who?"

"Andre."

"Me, too. I really need to meet this punk ass nigga who decided to put his hands on you. Maybe I can ask him if he'd like to try that shit on me."

"It's not like that."

"Not like what?"

"Like what you think."

"What am I thinking?"

Zola ignored him and walked over to the living room. She was looking around as if she were a crime scene investigator. Things were coming back to her now and the more she remembered the more she wished that she'd never met Andre.

The pain in her side shot a debilitating jolt to her and she winced and took a seat on the sofa.

"Zo," Ravon said. "What's going on?"

"What do you mean?" Zola asked as she rubbed her side gingerly.

"What's going on here? Who is this Andre guy?"

"Just a guy I know."

"Is this his place?"

"No," she said. "It's mine."

"Where do you work?"

"I don't."

"Then how can you afford a place like this?"

"Long story," she said.

"I got time."

"He bought it, but it's my place. My name is on the deed."

"And he gets to come around here and beat your ass when he feels like it? Is that part of the deal?"

If you only knew, she thought, but kept her mouth closed.

"It's not like that," Zola said.

"Stop saying that! What is it like then?" Ravon snapped.

Zola didn't respond. She pulled out her cell phone again and dialed Andre's number.

"Hello," a man's voice that didn't belong to Andre said.

"Hello," Zola said. "May I speak to Andre?"

"No," the man's voice replied.

"Who is this?" she asked.

"Zola," the voice said, "I want you to listen to me and listen very carefully."

"Who in the hell is this?"

"I'm talking," the voice said calmly.

Zola didn't respond. There was something about the man's tone that said he meant business.

"I want you to forget you ever met Andre. If anyone happens to ask you any questions about Andre, you are to tell them the truth. And the truth is, you haven't seen him since the last time he attacked you. Now if you don't do this and insist on asking questions, things can get bad for you in a hurry. Pretty simple, you keep your mouth closed and live, or run your mouth and it gets ugly. It's totally up to you."

"Who is this?"

"You're running your mouth," the voice said. "Now hang up the phone and enjoy your life."

Zola dropped her head. *What have I gotten myself into*, she wondered, and pushed the little red icon to end the call. She looked at her brother.

"This shit is getting weirder by the minute."

7

Ian rode on the back of the garbage truck, lost in his own thoughts. Walker was rambling on about something or another, but Ian wasn't hearing him. It had been a full week since he'd entered that man's condominium and killed him. Surprisingly, he wasn't worried about the repercussions of that crime anymore. There was something about his father getting involved that washed away any fear he had of going to jail. The only thing that bothered him now was the woman. He couldn't stop thinking about her and he wanted to know if she was okay. Did she survive? She was beaten pretty badly and she was unconscious when he dropped her off. The more he thought about it, the more he wished he would've taken her to a hospital instead of dropping her off on a porch somewhere in the middle of the hood. He did find a little comfort in the fact that whoever answered the door did get her into the house.

Ian had driven by that same house where he dropped the woman off at least ten times, but he couldn't bring himself to get out of his truck and knock on the door.

Just then, his cell phone rang. Ian looked at the caller ID. It was his sister, Andrea.

"Hello," he said, pushing the phone close to his ear so that he could hear over the noise of the garbage truck. "How's life treating you?"

"I've been better," she said. "What about you?"

"What's wrong?" he asked.

"The question is, what's wrong with you? I'm worried about you," she said. "You don't spend time with us no more. You keep my nephew away from me and that's not fair. I love him more than you give me credit for, but you won't let me or anyone else see him. That's selfish and uncalled for."

Ian held the phone to his ear. His sister had always been a drama queen, but she had a point.

"I'll make sure I do a better job of staying in touch."

"You always say that and nothing changes. No," Andrea said, "that's not gonna fly this time."

"What do you want me to do, Andrea?"

"I'm cooking dinner tonight and I want you guys to come over. Everyone will be here, including Daddy."

"I heard. What's the occasion?" he asked.

"It's a surprise. Besides why does it have to be a special occasion for family to get together?"

"It doesn't have to be anything special. I was just asking."

"I'm happy to have a family and I want to see you guys more often. So I'm not taking no for an answer. I expect to see you and Christian both."

"I don't know," he said. "I've had a long week. Maybe another time."

"Who hasn't had a long week, Ian? Come on. This would mean a lot to me. Malcolm is flying in from Seattle for the weekend. There, now you ruined the surprise."

"When did he move to Seattle?"

"Last year, Ian."

"Wow. I guess I'm out of the loop."

"Well, get back in it. Are you gonna come?"

Ian was quiet for a minute. He needed to get a life and maybe he could start with his family. "Yeah," he said. "We'll be there."

"Yayyyyy!" she screamed like a child on a roller coaster. "I can't wait. I haven't seen Christian since this past summer."

"Yeah," Ian said. "It has been a while."

"Well, I'm so looking forward to it. I'll see you around seven, okay?"

"That works for me. See you tonight," he said before hanging up.

"Who dat you talkin to, brodda? Some pretty gurl?"

"Yeah," Ian said with a smile. "She's lovely."

"Good for you, brodda. You gotta release your testicles every so often or you'll blow up and die. For true," Walker said, nodding his head rapidly to support his African myth.

Ian laughed.

"It's not a laughing matter. My wife said no more sex for two months. I feel like a dead man walking. If God didn't want you to use it, why would He put so much fire in de body? I'm going to get a girlfriend. De kind you pay money for. Dat way all of my problems will go away and I don't have to worry about getting a divorce. If Tiger Woods wasn't so cheap, he might be okay."

"Didn't you accuse your wife of cheating? How you gonna go out and cheat?"

"In my country, a man cannot cheat. As long as he can afford her, he's good to go and I can afford a woman on de side, brodda."

"Well, in this country, that'll get your dick chopped off," Ian said.

Walker frowned and instinctively grabbed his private part and almost fell off of the back of the truck.

Ian laughed again. It felt good to be laughing. It felt like he hadn't laughed so freely in years.

They pulled into Lake Kanawha, one of Atlanta's most expensive neighborhoods, and started emptying the trash cans. After clearing about five or six houses, a man called out to them as he ran up, dragging a can behind him. Ian hit the side of the truck to get the driver to stop.

Ian recognized him immediately, but the man didn't seem to know who he was.

He stared directly into the eyes of the man he thought he had killed.

Confused, Ian peered in for a closer look. Was his mind playing tricks on him? No, this was the guy. He never forgot a face and he was one-hundred percent sure this was the same guy, but the big man looked perfectly fine. No cuts, no bruises, nothing on his face to show that he had sustained a serious beatdown a week ago. And, up until this very moment, Ian actually thought he had killed the guy. His mind went back to the scene of the crime and he visualized the big man lying on the floor with his nose split wide open, while he struggled to pull his pants up. The man's nose was bleeding profusely and had a nasty gash on the bridge. At the very least, he should've had a scratch to show for his troubles, but this man's face was smooth as a baby's bottom.

"Hey," the man said, "I'm sorry to hold you guys up but I forgot today was trash day. I already missed it last week. This crap has been in my garage and it's starting to stink."

"No problem, brodda," Walker said. "You right on time."

Ian stared at the man and wondered what kind of magical healing herbs he was sipping on. A part of him wanted to jump off the back of the truck and reintroduce himself for the ill deeds he had done to that woman, but the smarter part of him made him simply nod his head when the man made eye contact.

Walker took the can from the man, emptied it, and handed it back to him.

"Have a blessed day, fellas," the man said with an easy smile as if he were the nicest man in the world. He reached into his pocket and removed his wallet.

Walker smiled, but Ian couldn't stop thinking about how this guy had pointed a gun at him in the middle of a busy street after beating a woman half to death.

"I'm glad I caught you. I sure didn't want to spend a few more days with this stench in my garage so I appreciate you waiting. And I know time is money so…" he said as he removed two twenty dollar bills and handed them to Walker.

"Thank you, my brodda," Walker said, slipping the money into his pocket and jumping back onto the truck. "God loves a cheerful giver."

"Y'all take care of yourselves," the man said and turned and jogged back up his driveway.

The truck pulled off and Ian watched as the big man disappeared back into the garage of a high-priced home. He couldn't help but wonder if he had a wife and kids inside. He bet she had no idea he was running around across town beating up women.

"Here ya go," Walker said, handing him one of the twenties. "Nothing makes my day like generosity."

"You go ahead and keep that, Walker," Ian said, still staring at the man's home.

"You must be wealthy, brodda. I don't turn down nuttin' but my collar," Walker said, as he laughed and put the money back into his pocket.

Ian made a mental note of the man's address. He kept his eye on the trash bag and wondered what was inside. He knew this wasn't his business and he should leave it alone but that wasn't going to happen. He was coming back.

8

After lying around her condo for four days, Zola realized she wasn't getting any better. Rest alone wasn't going to heal her. She reached for her cell phone and dialed her brother's number.

Yo, this is your boy, Ravon. I'm on my grind right now but leave me a message and I will holla back. Beeep.

"Ravon," Zola said, barely able to speak. "This is Zola. I need for you to come and take me to the hospital. You know I can't do ambulances."

She hung up the phone and grimaced as she swung her legs over the side of the bed. She stood up and felt a little dizzy.

The sun was peeking around the blinds and into her bedroom. She looked at the clock and discovered it was already nine in the morning. She found her balance and walked to the bathroom. With each step she took, it felt like someone was stabbing her in the ribs with a long needle. She sat down on the toilet to relieve herself but something didn't feel right. As Zola looked down between her legs, what she saw down in the water almost scared the life out of her. The toilet bowl was now a crimson red as her blood splattered all over the white porcelain. Trembling with fear, she stood and moved away from the blood until her back was against the wall. She stared at the blood like it was death itself, then looked up to the ceiling as if God had some answers to the million-and-one questions running around her head. Zola took a deep breath but felt her stomach turn. She rushed over to the toilet and threw up. Finally able to momentarily regain her composure, she flushed the toilet and walked over to the sink to rinse out her mouth.

Zola made it back to her bedroom and picked up her cell phone. She scrolled through the address book on her BlackBerry and realized that she didn't have anyone she could call. All of her associates were either friends of Andre or people she did business with, such as the dry cleaner, plumber, hairstylist etc. She had been completely cut off from any form of a social life since she started dealing with Andre. Finally, out of options, she found the number to the front office and got Kecia on the line.

"Kecia," she said. "This is Zola. I really need your help."

"Hey, Zola. Are you okay? What do you need?"

"I need to go to the hospital," Zola said, hoping she sounded calmer than she felt.

"What's going on? Should I call an ambulance?"

"No, I hate ambulances," Zola said. "I was wondering if you could take me?"

"Ok, sure, but I'll have to find somebody to cover for me. Can you give me a few minutes?" Kecia asked.

"I feel like I'm dying, but I can't get in an ambulance," she managed through clenched teeth.

"Okay," Kecia said. "Hold tight. I'll be right up."

"Thank you, Kecia. I owe you big time," Zola said. "I'm throwing up and urinating blood."

"Oh, my God. Maybe I should call an ambulance, Zola. That sounds serious."

"No, just get here as soon as you can."

"Will do," Kecia said before hanging up.

Less than ten minutes later, Kecia was standing over Zola's bed, looking down at a woman who was barely hanging on.

"Oh, my God," Kecia said. "What in the world happened to you?"

Zola struggled to her feet and Kecia ran over to assist her before she fell down. Kecia helped Zola over to the sofa while she looked around for something for her to wear to the hospital.

"I wish I knew," Zola said, frustrated that she still had no recollection of what had happened.

"Why didn't you call me sooner?"

"I don't know."

"Well, let's get you to a doctor," Kecia said. She found a house robe hanging on the foot rail of the bed and slid it on Zola's fragile body. She looked around and grabbed Zola's purse, then helped her get to her feet.

Somehow they made it down the hallway, down the elevator and out to Kecia's car. Kecia drove a Mini Cooper and the passenger seat was filled with clothes and the already small rear seat was taken up with two large boxes.

"Oh doggone it. I forgot I had all of this stuff in my car," Kecia said. "I had to move out of my place last night."

"We can take my car," Zola said as she started walking down the garage toward her Jaguar.

Kecia led Zola over to the car and eased her down into the passenger seat. She closed the door, rushed around to the driver's side and jumped in. After buckling up, she eased out of the parking garage and headed toward Crawford Long Medical facility.

"Zola," Kecia said as she moved into the HOV lane on I-20 West. "What happened to you? You said you didn't remember, but surely you remember something?"

"I keep hoping this is a bad dream, but I know it's not," Zola said, wincing in pain. She was tired of the pain and for the first time in a long time, she wished that she was dead.

"I see," Kecia said. "I really like to mind my own business. I swear to God I do, because I have enough problems of my own. But, when I saw you walk into the lobby the other day…my heart broke into a million little pieces."

"The temp who was working for me a few days ago called and told me she saw you running in the street trying to get away from Mr. Harris. I didn't believe her at first but then you came in and I realized she was telling the truth. Before, I always ignored the rumors when other tenants would come down and say how they could hear you screaming when they were walking down the halls. But, now…"

Zola felt embarrassed to hear these words, but she was in too much pain to really care.

"That's why I was actually happy when those men came to get his ass," Kecia said.

Zola's ears perked up and she looked at Kecia.

"What men?"

"It was three of them. They came to me and got the videotapes from the garage, and then they went and got him. He was crying like a baby, too. Mumbling something about how he would tell them everything. I'm like 'tell them what?' I've been around men like Mr. Harris my entire life. They can give it, but they can't take it."

"What men are you talking about? Who took Andre? Were they police officers?"

"I don't know, but I don't think so, and after seeing you like this, I really don't care."

Zola thought back to the warning she had gotten from the man who'd called and figured she'd better learn to think like Kecia or she would find herself in worse shape than she was already in.

"You're gonna be okay, Zola," Kecia said. "We're almost there."

Zola nodded her head as she let the seat all the way back so that she had less pressure on her aching ribs.

Then her cell phone rang.

"You wanna get that?" Kecia asked.

Zola nodded her head and Kecia reached into the back seat to retrieve Zola's purse. She fiddled around inside the purse while she used her left hand to steer the vehicle.

"Here," she said, handing the phone to Zola.

Zola looked at the screen and it said private. She hit the green icon as she said hello.

"Hi, Mom," Jason's lively voice said on the other end of the line.

Zola's heart rate increased and she tried to sit up, but a painful jolt in her sides forced her to stay put.

"Hey, buddy," she said, trying to sound as normal as possible.

"How are you, Mom?"

"I'm good. Actually, I'm on my way to the hospital."

"Hospital?" Jason asked, sounding more mature than he had the last time they spoke. "Why?"

"I was in a bad car accident," Zola lied.

"Oh no," Jason said. "Which hospital? I'm going to see if my mom or dad will bring me there to see you."

Zola loved to hear her son's voice on the other end of the telephone and when he called her "mom" that was even sweeter, but when she heard him refer to another woman as "mom," somehow that bothered her. She had all the respect in the world for the Benjamins. They were very good people and she really appreciated the fact that they were giving her son a better life than any she could've ever imagined, but she wanted that "mom" title to be hers and hers alone.

"I'm going to Crawford Long. Are you going to try and come see me?"

"Yes," Jason said. "What happened?"

"A car pulled out in front of me," she said, still lying, and hating every minute of it.

"I'll call you back in a little while. Let me get my mom on the phone," he said.

"Okay," she said. "I love you."

"I love you, too," he said before hanging up.

"That was my son." Zola smiled, realizing that the mere sound of his voice made her happy to be alive.

9

ola was seen and examined by a doctor not long after she arrived in the emergency room. The physician suggested that she be admitted right away. She was wheeled to a room on a gurney and given a nightgown to change into. She had a private room and thanked God for her insurance. Moments after she was settled, there was a knock on her door.

"Hey," Kecia said, peeking her head into the room.

"Hey," Zola said as she pulled the covers up around her neck. "You're still here?"

"Yeah," Kecia said as she walked in the room and stood beside Zola's bed. "Did you think I would leave you here all alone? I'm appalled."

Zola smiled. "Thanks for everything, Kecia. I really appreciate you. Whatever they gave me is working. I'm feeling a little better already."

"Good," Kecia said.

"You don't have to stay here. You have better things to do than to hang around a hospital with me."

"I'm okay," Kecia said, looking down at her battered friend. "So what's the word on your condition?"

"Broken ribs, internal bleeding, and a few other things that I couldn't pronounce," Zola said, shaking her head. "They gave me something for the pain and now I see how folks get hooked on prescription meds. I'm feeling nice," she said with a smile. "The doctor said he has to run some more tests, so I may be here for a few days."

"Wow," Kecia said. "I hope you're going to leave him. I don't like to mind other people's business, but since you involved me, I feel like I can state my opinion."

"He's not a bad guy," Zola said.

"What?!" Kecia almost screamed. "Well, what does he have to do for you to think he's a bad guy? Kill you?"

"No," Zola said. "You don't understand."

"You know what, Zola," Kecia said, shaking her head. "Don't be that chick."

"What chick?"

"That one who makes excuses for a man who whips her ass. Under no circumstance are you to be used as a punching bag."

"I hear ya," Zola said, giving up on explaining anything to her well-meaning friend.

Kecia looked at her and shook her head. She had seen this so many times with the prostitutes she grew up with.

"Did you call your brother?"

"Not since I left home. Can you hand me my phone out of my purse?"

Kecia walked over and got the phone.

Before Zola could dial the number, she noticed the screen had five missed calls. She called her voicemail and heard four different messages from Jason. He didn't sound happy when he told her he couldn't make it to the hospital. He then said something that she hadn't heard since he went to live with the Benjamins three years ago. He told her he wanted to come home, home being back with her. Zola sat up and dialed the number to the Benjamins' home.

"Hello," Chad Benjamin said.

"Hi, Chad," Zola said. "How are you?"

"I'm well," he said in his ever-chipper voice. "How's life treating you?"

"Not so good. I was in a car accident," she said, continuing the lie.

"Oh no," Chad said. "Are you going to be okay?"

"I think so."

"Well, if you need anything, please don't hesitate to call," he said with genuine concern. "You know we are here for you."

Zola had always had a great relationship with the Benjamins. They were a white couple, living in a wealthy white world, yet they took in her black child with open arms.

"Thank you," she said. "Is Jason around?"

"No," Chad said. "Carmen took him someplace. I'm not sure where they went."

"Humm. Okay," Zola said. "Well, tell him that I'm at Crawford Long."

"Crawford Long? Must've been some accident. Are you sure you're okay?" Chad asked.

"Yeah," she said. "I'll be fine. Jason said he was going to ask Carmen to bring him up here to see me, but then he left a message saying he couldn't come."

"Really?" Chad said. "That's odd. I'll have to get her on the phone to see what's going on."

"Okay. I have my cell phone with me, so if you don't mind, tell him to call me. I would love to hear his voice."

"Okay," Chad said. "I will pass along the message and you get better soon."

"Thank you," she said and ended the call. She placed the phone on her chest, wondering what was going on with her son.

"Is your son okay?" Kecia asked.

"I hope so. He left me a message and said he wants to come back and live with me."

"Is that a good thing or a bad thing?" Kecia asked, fishing since she wasn't in the know.

"It's a great thing. I have been trying to get myself together so he could come back home, but something in his voice didn't sound right."

"Do you have any pictures of him?" Kecia asked.

Zola picked up her phone and scrolled through the photos. "He sends me stuff all the time," she said as she handed Kecia her BlackBerry.

"He's handsome," Kecia said, scrolling through the pictures. She stopped at a family portrait with Jason and his adopted family. "Who are these white people in the picture?"

"Those are the people he lives with," Zola said.

"I know this lady," Kecia said, staring at the white woman with the short, red hair. "She looks very familiar. I never forget a face. I don't know where I know her from, but it'll come to me."

"That's Carmen," Zola said, rolling her eyes, "Jason's 'step-mom.' She's always on television. She does something with the school board or something political. I'm not sure. Are you sure you don't have anything to do? I'm enjoying your company, but I don't want to keep you."

"My shift is over and I don't have class tonight. I need to study but I also need to find a new apartment. I had to bail out of my place last night. Those Negroes were out there shooting at each other like they live in the Wild, Wild West or someplace. The last thing I need is to catch a stray bullet. I have places to be in life and I refuse to let ghetto Negroes ruin it by shooting me in my head," she said.

"Wow," Zola said.

"There is a reason why poor folks stay poor. They would rather kill each other than learn a doggone trade, but like I said, I refuse to let them kill me. I've been through too much to let somebody who is nobody kill me," Kecia said as she continued to study the face of the white woman on Zola's phone. "I know this woman, Zola, and it's not from television."

"Well, if you think of it, let me know. She's okay. A little judg-mental at times, but her heart's in the right place."

Kecia hit a few buttons and forwarded the picture to her cell phone. Her lawyer instincts were racing. Something wasn't right and you could read that all over her face. Once she was done, she handed Zola's phone back to her.

A nurse walked in, nodded her head at Kecia, and checked the machine that was hooked up to Zola.

"No cell phones are allowed. They mess with the radio waves in the sensors," the nurse said as she pushed a few more buttons on the monitor. "Sorry, but you can have your loved ones call you on the room phone."

"Okay, no problem," Zola said.

Kecia reached out for the phone and Zola handed it to her.

The nurse left and Kecia offered the phone back to her but Zola shook her head. "If my son calls, give him the number off of that phone right there. I don't need to have anything breaking that will have me staying here longer."

Kecia looked at the room phone and punched the number into her own cell.

"Well, Kecia, you are more than welcome to stay at my place. It's not like I'll be there for a few days. Even if I was, you could still stay," Zola said.

"For real? Cool, because I'm broke as a joke. I do not have the money for another deposit and first and last month's rent, which is what everybody seems to want," Kecia said.

There was a knock on the door, and then it opened before Zola could say a word.

Two plainclothes police officers entered the room. Both of them showed their credentials before speaking.

"Are you Zola Zaire?" the tall, white officer asked in an official tone.

"Yes," she said.

Kecia took that as her cue to leave. She squeezed Zola's hand and whispered that she would call her. Zola nodded and waited for her to exit the room.

"What's the problem?" she asked.

"We are investigating a murder," the black officer said.

"A murder?" Zola frowned as her heart began to race. "Who was murdered?"

"Sara Zaire was found dead today. She was stabbed thirty-three times," the white officer said with the casualness of someone who was ordering lunch at the local McDonald's.

"What?" Zola said as she tried to sit up. "My mother? You're telling me that my mother was murdered?"

"Yes," the white guy said with little, if any, emotion.

"When?"

"We found her today," the white guy said. "And it is my understanding that you were the last person seen leaving her house. Care to have a few words with us?"

10

Ian stepped out of the shower and walked into his modest bedroom. He looked around the small room and sighed. His king-sized bed sat in the middle of the room and left very little space for a dresser and a night stand. Lately he had been finding everything wrong with his house and neighborhood. Before, nothing mattered. Now, the kitchen was too cramped; the closets didn't hold all of his clothes; his son's bathroom was too this; or his living room was too that. He glanced at a pile of real estate magazines he had picked up but never read, then made a mental note to take a look at a few of them when he made it back home tonight. Maybe he and Christian could go house hunting this weekend.

He was even excited about his dinner tonight with his family. He had practically cut everyone off after the loss of his wife and daughter, but now he felt it was time to move on. He sat on his bed with his body still covered with water drops, picked up his family portrait, and stared at his daughter's bright smile. She looked like a miniature version of his wife. Ian's eyes moved over to meet his wife's eyes and he couldn't help but smile. He loved her with everything he had. He shook his head and refused to allow himself to fall back into the trap of asking why. That line of thinking never got him anywhere. His gaze shifted back to his little girl and his smile faded. He missed her but he had cried so many tears that he didn't have any more left. He held the picture up to his lips and kissed it. Instead of placing it back on the nightstand, he opened the drawer and placed it inside. It was time to move on, if not for his own sanity, for Christian's.

He realized that in the process of mourning his family, he wasn't allowing his son to live his life to the fullest. His son had been begging him to teach him how to play basketball, and all he ever did was put it off for another day. That had yet to come. It was almost as if he and Christian were living in a bubble and the rest of the world didn't really exist. He realized how completely self-centered his actions were, but his mourning wouldn't allow him to get out of his own way and let his child have some fun. Something had to give, which became painfully clear when he picked Christian up from daycare. Once he shared their plans for the evening with his son, Christian started smiling from ear to ear and talking non-stop about a family that he barely knew.

Ian stood, walked over to his dresser, pulled out his undergarments and slid them on. He leaned out into the hallway to sneak a peek at his son who was already pacing. He was past ready to go.

"Hey, man," Ian said. "You got yourself dressed?"

"Yes," Christian said, standing up to show off his black jeans, a T-shirt with a cartoon character of a large red dog on it, and a fireman's hat.

Any other time, Ian would send him back to his room and make him change his clothes, but he was burying that guy.

"You are one sharp dude, Mr. DeMarco," he said, smiling and shaking his head.

Christian frowned as if he wasn't expecting that and then smiled. "I can wear it, Daddy?"

"Sure," Ian said. "I don't see why not. You look good in your fireman's hat."

"Thank you," Christian said before sitting down on the floor to play with his cars.

Ian walked back into his room and picked up the remote control for the television. He turned the volume up on the news and opened the door of his closet to find something to wear. His eyes jerked toward the screen when he heard:

An Atlanta woman is being questioned regarding the apparent murder of Sara Zaire. The woman in question is being treated at Crawford Long Medical Center and is recovering from injuries in what authorities are calling a lover's quarrel gone wrong.

Ian's eyes grew big as the woman's face popped up on the screen. He knew that face.

Authorities are saying the victim lived in this house and that she was the mother of the alleged perpetrator. The woman in question, Zola Zaire, has a history of violence against her mother, but there is more. The victim, Sara Zaire, was convicted and spent time in prison for crimes against the very person whose murder she is now being questioned about. A very interesting case of family violence. You heard it first here and we will continue to keep you updated. I'm Samantha James, Channel Seven News at Six.

Ian recognized the house on the television as the same one where he had dropped off the beaten woman. He scratched his head and decided he had already done his job.

He quickly got dressed, turned the television off and walked out of the room.

"Let's go, li'l buddy," Ian said.

As Ian and Christian walked out on the front porch, they heard gunshots. Ian pushed his son back into the house and told him to go to his room and lay down. Ian retrieved his own gun from his bedroom and walked back to the living room. He peeked out of the window and scanned the street for signs of danger. Could someone be coming for him or was it the local thugs being themselves? After a few minutes, he stepped outside and looked around.

The area drunks, Willie and Harry, were standing across the street arguing about something, seemingly oblivious to the gunshots that had been heard minutes ago.

"Niggero, Barack Obama ain't the president. The white man put him up front to shut yo' dumb ass up," Willie said as he took a swig of his liquor straight from the bottle. "George Bush and all them other crackers still running thangs."

"You know you 'bout an ignant sumbitch," Harry said, shaking his head. "The white man ain't never gave two stankin' cents about what black folks be talking about. So why all of a sudden would they wanna shut us up? And they damn sure ain't going so far as to make a black man president to shut us up. Give the brother his due; he outsmarted they asses, and now he in the big house, sitting at the big desk, doing big things."

"First of all, he ain't Black, so stop calling him a brother," Willie said.

"You a fool. Obama is Black; his daddy is blacker than yo' daddy."

"So the hell what?"

"And guess what else? He looks good in a suit," Harry countered. "I'm happy, damn it."

"Bull crap! He ain't no brother. Him and Tiger Woods got the same shit going on with they bloodlines. The white man ain't gonna give no real nigga that job. Trust me on that one," Willie said.

"I wouldn't trust you with a boiled egg and a sock with no match. Hell, the *black* man wouldn't give a nigga no job. And you should know, nigga. When the last time you had one? The world don't like niggas and I don't either. Niggas kill grass."

"You damn right. I'm a nigga and proud of it. But you better watch your damn mouth, Harry," Willie snapped. "I'm 'bout tired of the insults. I'll take this damn sword out and chop your damn head off. Try me."

"Man, you and that rusty ass sword can go to hell."

"Keep on and I'mma put my foot so far in your ass your breath gonna smell like my shoe polish," Willie said.

"Willie," Harry said with a frown. "Negro, if you ever dream about putting your raggedy-ass dick beaters on me, you better wake up and apologize. 'Cause I will knock the pure dee snot outta yo ass."

"You and what army?" Willie said, taking another drink of his liquor before handing it to Harry.

"What's up, fellas?" Ian asked, walking up between the two alcoholics who argued to pass the time every day, all day. "Did y'all see who was out here shooting?"

"Hell no," Willie said. "But I sure wish whoever did it would come 'round here and put one or two in this fool. Dumb sumbitch."

"I ain't gonna be too many more bitches now," Harry warned. "I'm tellin' you now. Keep it up and it ain't gonna be pretty."

"Man," Ian said with a slight chuckle. "Why can't ya'll get along?"

"Cause I can't fool with an ignant ass nigga. I don't like niggas, Ian," Harry said as if he was really frustrated with the man he spent his every waking moment with. "And this one right here might as well be called Chief Nigga."

"What make you any better than me, Harry?" Willie snapped.

"My mind," Harry said, slapping himself hard in the temple. "That's what. I got a degree, fool. I grew up…"

"Oh, shut the hell up," Willie said, cutting him off. "Don't nobody wanna hear about what the hell you used to do. Yo' ass is out here with me every damn day and I quit school in the eighth grade. You think because you went to some old-ass college two hundred years ago with Frederick Douglas, that you better than me?"

"You know what, Ian? It gets on my last nerve to see a black man who won't give another black man his proper due," Harry said. "That's why we can't have shit."

"Ian," Willie said, interrupting Harry. "You seem to be a decent man with a good head on your shoulders. Well, when you ain't walking round here with your ass on your face. But anyway, let me ask you a question. Do you think Barack Obama is really the president?"

"Huh?" Ian asked.

"Huh, hell," Willie said. "You heard me, nukka. Or do you think he's just a front man? I believe the white man still calling the shots."

"Yeah, Willie, he's the president," Ian said, shooting a quick glance back at his house to make sure his son was okay. "And he's smart enough to call his own shots."

"Damn," Willie said, shaking his head from side to side as if he had heard some grave news.

"I can't believe you even asked somebody that dumb question. It's better to let folks think you're stupid than to open your dumb mouth and remove all doubt," Harry said. "You don't care who knows how ignant yo' ass is, do you, Willie?"

"Both of you sumbitches stupid as hell," Willie said, reaching over to Harry. "Give me my got damn bottle back."

Ian shook his head. "A'ight guys. Y'all try to be careful out here," he said as he walked back across the street to his house. He opened the door and called out to Christian. The little boy ran to his father and they jumped into Ian's truck.

Once he was in the car, Ian switched his radio to News Talk

with hopes of hearing something else about the woman whose face was plastered across his television screen. He didn't know her, but something was telling him that she was getting a raw deal. He was willing to bet his last dollar that the abusive man was the one behind the killing. After all, she was in no condition to even walk, much less kill.

But what about his father? Could one of his people be responsible for this? His father did say that he would take care of it.

Ian quickly tossed the thought from his mind. His father was a lot of things, but reckless wasn't one of them. Especially after the family tragedy that changed them all.

Ian tried to think of something else, but as he drove along, his thoughts kept going back to that woman. He could see her in his mind, sitting in a cell all alone. He felt a twinge of fear, guilt, and compassion for her. The probability of the police showing up to talk to him increased dramatically with these new developments, yet that wasn't what bothered him most. He was more concerned about the woman.

"Hunh, Daddy?"

Ian's mind had raced so much that he didn't realize he was ignoring his son.

"What was that, buddy?" he asked.

"Can we spend the night?"

"No, we can't spend the night, but we can stay real late though. How about that?"

"Okay," Christian said, still sounding a bit disappointed, but pacified by the fact that he would be spending lots of time with his family.

They pulled into the driveway of his sister's high-priced subdivision and stopped at a small house that stood at the security gate.

"Wow," Christian said, pointing at a huge brick house sitting on a hill. "I wanna live in that house."

"That is nice, huh?" Ian said.

"Yeah. Look at that one, Daddy," Christian said, pointing to another one. "When I get rich, Daddy, I'mma buy us one."

"That's good to know," Ian said as he handed the security guard his identification. "I'm here to see my sister, Andrea Marion."

"Yes, sir, Mr. DeMarco," the guard, who looked like an old Will Smith, said with a pleasant smile. "Your name is on her guest list. Do you know how to get to her place?"

"Yes," Ian said. "It's been a minute, but I think I remember."

"She's on this street all the way at the end of the cul-de-sac," he said.

"Thanks," Ian said and pulled off. He felt butterflies in his stomach as he approached his sister's huge stucco home. He saw the long Lincoln Town Car which meant that his father had already arrived. A few other cars were in the driveway and he pulled up behind one, killed his ignition, and took a deep breath. He looked back at his son who returned his stare with a big smile.

"Let's go see the family," Ian said and felt good about his first step back to the way things were.

11

"As it stands right now, Ms. Zaire, you haven't been officially charged with any crime at all," Homicide Detective Errol Shilo said. Detective Shilo was about five feet ten inches tall, black as coal and had muscles everywhere. His shiny, bald head seemed to glow when he moved a certain way under the fluorescent ceiling lights. His partner, Detective Lester Sullivan, was the physical opposite. He was tall, Caucasian, rail thin, and had a head full of gray hair.

"However," Detective Sullivan said, playing the bad cop, "you are our prime suspect. There is no doubt about that."

Zola stared at the man, thinking he would break out laughing and tell her this was all some cruel joke. He returned her glare with a stony face, letting her know that this was far from a joke.

"I didn't murder anybody," Zola said. "And I don't appreciate ya'll coming in here accusing me of it either."

"We're not accusing you of anything, Ms. Zaire. We're investigating a crime and you are a suspect. No more, no less," Shilo said.

"You really don't seem all that bothered by the news that your mother is dead. Why is that? Could it be that you helped send her to the afterlife?" Detective Sullivan asked.

"I didn't send her anywhere," Zola snapped.

"Look at you. You're pretty cold and nonchalant. If someone told me my mother was murdered, I'd be a complete wreck," Sullivan said.

"Good for you," she spat.

"So why did you do it?" Detective Sullivan asked.

"Why did I do what?" she asked.

"Why did you murder your mother?"

"Didn't I tell you I didn't murder anybody? I'm not confessing to a crime so you lazy bastards can cross it off of your to-do list. Screw y'all; do your investigation."

"What kind of relationship did you have with your mother?" Detective Shilo asked in a soft tone, playing his good cop role to a tee.

"There wasn't a relationship. I didn't like her and she didn't like me. I hate it that someone killed her, but I didn't have anything to do with it. My mother is, or was, a bitch, but I would never do anything to harm her," Zola said.

"So you didn't like your mother?" Sullivan interjected.

"Are you deaf?" she said. "What part of what I just said did you not understand?"

"Why were you guys arguing?" Shilo asked.

"I don't recall us arguing," Zola said.

"Your neighbor," Sullivan said, pausing to flip through his notepad, "Mrs. Ham, said she heard you guys yelling at each other. Then she saw you rushing out of the house. Why were you in such a hurry to leave?"

"She told me to get out," Zola said dryly.

"Do you mind telling us what happened to your face?" Shilo asked.

"I don't recall," Zola said unconvincingly.

"Could that be from the struggle? Could it be that Sara fought you with everything she had, yet you still plunged your knife into her? Not just once, not twice, but thirty-three times? You stuck that knife into your mother over and over and over until she lay dead. That's what happened. Why don't you admit it? If you confess, maybe we can work with you. If not, then you take the chance of spending the rest of your life in prison."

Zola sighed as if this entire scene was more of a nuisance than anything. She tuned the men out and tried to dig deep into her soul to find something that would make her feel bad about her mother's demise, but there was nothing there.

"Hello... Over here," Detective Sullivan said, waving his hand in Zola's face to get her attention.

"What?" she said, shooting the detective a cold stare.

"Why where you over at your mother's house?" Sullivan asked.

"Don't know," Zola said.

"You don't know?" Sullivan said. "Well, you do have the right to remain silent but I wish you would help us out. I mean, because as of right now, my thinking is that you're a cold-blooded killer, Ms. Zaire. And I believe you finished the job that you started when you were a little girl."

"Do you even know what really happened when I was a little girl?" Zola said.

"Sure," Detective Sullivan said. "I have it right here in my little pad. It says you stabbed your mother and her boyfriend who you were having an affair with."

Zola shook her head in sad disbelief.

"Was there anyone else at your mother's house that you know of?" Detective Shilo asked.

"No," Zola said. She wouldn't dare mention her brother's name, even though she couldn't help but wonder how or if he fit into this whole scenario. He had yet to return her phone calls, which was strange considering how much concern he had shown for her when they had last seen each other. "I don't even know how I got there. I woke up in my old room. My mother walked in, screaming about how I had to get my stuff together and get out; so I got my bag and left. When I left her house, she was sitting on the sofa watching some television show."

"What show?" Shilo asked. "Do you remember?"

"One of those court T.V. judge shows," Zola said. "*Judge Joe Brown* or *Judge Judy* or something. I can't say for certain."

"So tell me," Detective Sullivan said. "You said you didn't remember how you got to your mother's house. What else don't you remember?"

"Now that has to be the stupidest question I've ever heard. Are you sure you're a detective?" Zola asked.

The officer shot her an icy glare and continued. "Let me rephrase the question. Do you think you would remember killing your mother?"

"I think I might remember that," Zola replied sarcastically.

"My investigation tells me—and you confirm it—that there was a great deal of resentment toward your mother. Did all of this start because she broke up the little fling you had going with her man? Then the father of your child mysteriously kills himself. Death seems to follow you wherever you go, Ms. Zaire."

"Rapes!" Zola snapped. "Both of them were rapes. One an outright rape and the other was statutory. Why are you in here harassing me? Why don't you get out of here and go out there and arrest some of those rapists who prey on young girls instead of sitting here blaming me? Do you know how old I was when I had my son? Hunh? Do you know how old his father was? Is that in your li'l pad?"

"If that's the case, then why didn't you ever call the authorities?" Sullivan asked.

"Because most of the authorities are just like your stupid ass," Zola said as she felt her temperature rise, thinking about what had happened to her as a child. "I think it's time I speak to an attorney," Zola said.

"Well," Detective Sullivan said with a smile, "Ms. Zaire, you certainly have the right to an attorney. But, you best believe that this is not over. I'm sure we're on the right track, so we will be back."

"Yeah, well, good luck," Zola said. "The fact that I was at my mother's house isn't reason enough for you to charge me with murder, you idiots!"

"Maybe not. But when you add that to the fact that you have motive, opportunity, and a very nasty disposition about you, there might be enough there," Detective Sullivan said with a wicked smile, as if nothing gave him more pleasure than to send a person to one of Georgia's prisons. "You're not under arrest yet, but it's coming. I would suggest you hire a good lawyer."

Zola's heart dropped down to the floor. Even in death, her mother was still causing her pain.

Detective Shilo wore a pained expression on his face as if he didn't agree with his partner. He stood and nodded at her as they left the room.

12

I an and Christian stood on the large wraparound porch of his sister's palatial estate and rang the doorbell. Seconds later, the door flew open and Andrea stood in her large foyer with an even larger smile on her face.

"Well, well, well, look at you guys," Andrea said, reaching down to hug her nephew. "Hi, Christian."

"Hi," he said shyly from the hiding spot behind his father's leg.

"You don't have to hide from me. I'm Auntie Andrea and I loveeeeee you," she said, drawing a smile from the little boy. "And listen. That fireman's hat is so cool. Are you going to be a fireman when you grow up?"

"Yes," Christian said, smiling but still holding on to Ian's leg.

"Well, that's great," Andrea said, then turned her attention to Ian and gave him a hug. "Hello, stranger. Y'all come on in. Christian, did I tell you that you are one handsome dude?"

"Thank you," Christian said with a wide smile.

Ian smiled too and once they were inside, he reached out and gave his sister another tight and long overdue hug. He felt himself getting emotional so he released his embrace.

"It's okay," Andrea said, wiping away her own tears. Ian's self-imposed exile from the family seemed to hurt her the most. They were always the closest of all of the siblings and when Ian cut the family off, she suffered the most. "I'm so happy to see you two handsome devils. Go on in to the living room. The gang's all here."

Ian walked in and immediately felt the nostalgia. It was like one big family reunion. His father was asleep by the fireplace. He had a half-finished beer in one hand and a newspaper in the other one. His brother, Malcolm, whom he hadn't seen in years, was holding a remote control and flicking through family videos.

"What in the world?" Malcolm said as he dropped the remote and stared at his big brother. He grinned and rushed over to grab the man who was his childhood protector and placed him in a bear hug. "Man, it's good to see you. And when did this li'l fella get so big? Oh, my God. Hey, Christian."

"Hi," Christian said shyly to the man he could only remember from pictures.

Malcolm was always called the crybaby of the bunch because he was always such a sensitive kid. And it seemed that getting older hadn't changed his emotional state. Tears streamed down his face as he stared at his nephew and big brother, shaking his head and trying to keep his emotions in check.

"Now don't you go crying, Malcolm," Ian said as he rubbed his brother's head just as he did when he was a kid.

"Man, hush." Malcolm nodded his head toward an Asian woman who was sitting on the sofa. "That's my wife, Ming."

"Wife?" Ian asked. "You found somebody willing to spend more than a few hours with you?"

"Shut up, man. I sent you an invitation to the wedding, but your sorry butt didn't even respond. You could've sent a note or something. Anyway, Ming, this is my big brother, Ian. He's the butt wipe I told you about."

Ming, short with long black hair and a baby doll face, stood and bowed to Ian. "Heard much about you. Good things. No butt wipe stuff," she said with a smile. "Nice to meet you, Ian."

"It's nice to meet you, too, Ming. This is my son, Christian."

"Handsome boy," Ming said, reaching out to touch Christian's hand.

Christian smiled politely and shook her hand.

"Such a gentleman," Ming said. "Looks just like a smaller version of his father."

"Man," Malcolm said butting in. "Why didn't you return my calls? You don't do family like that, dude."

"All I can say is, I'm sorry," Ian said, holding his hands out to his sides. "And please wipe those tears off of your face. You're gonna let your wife see you crying."

Malcolm twisted his lip. "Yeah. She knows I'm sensitive. That's part of my sex appeal. I keep it real. I'm happy to see you, big bro," Malcolm said, reaching out for another hug.

"Man, move," Ian said, pushing his brother away. "I've been here five minutes and you've already hugged me five times. Go on back over there and play with your videos."

"Oh, you gonna act like that," Malcolm said, fanning his brother away. "Fine. I see you still have an attitude problem."

Christian looked around at the room full of strangers who were all smiling at him. He noticed his grandfather sleeping in the chair. He zeroed in on him and took off running. He stopped, planted, and leaped up on his grandfather's lap.

"Ouch," Colin said with a loud grunt. He opened his eyes and frowned. Once his eyes adjusted to the little brown face smiling back at him, he returned a smile of his own. "Christian," he said. "Boy, you gonna break one of your granddaddy's bones."

"Hey, Granddaddy," he said. "I got my car with me. You wanna play?"

"Boy, you get right down to business, don't cha?" Colin said with a smile. He rubbed his grandson's head, lifted him up and placed Christian back down in his chair. "We'll take care of that playing in just a second. Let your granddaddy take a bathroom break."

Colin walked over to Ian. He stopped in front of his son and extended his hand. "Nice to see ya, son."

Ian looked at the hand. Everyone in the room watched, fully aware of the rift between the two men.

"Nice to see you, too," Ian said, smiling and pushing away his father's hand. He pulled the old man in for a tight embrace. He held his father a long time, trying to make up for the years they were separated by circumstance.

"Oh, now you wanna get all mushy. Is this Ian or Malcolm?"

"Why y'all wanna get on me just because I don't hide my feelings?" Malcolm asked.

"Hush, Malcolm," Colin said as his watery eyes told how he really felt. "Let me go to the bathroom, boy. I'm not as young as I used to be. That beer got my bladder working over-time. Andrea, you're supposed to hide the beer from me when I come over here."

"Do you need for me to run out and get you some Depends, Pops?" Ian joked, surprised as anyone else that he had picked up his old personality without a hitch.

"I might," Colin said with a chuckle before making his way to the hallway bathroom.

"I'm so happy you did that," Andrea said. "He really needed that. You were always his favorite."

"I thought *I* was his favorite," Malcolm said, looking serious.

"You are his favorite. Ever since he took you from those crackheads," Ian said with a straight face.

"What crackheads?" Malcolm asked.

Ian put his hand over his mouth. "Oh, Lord, I done said too much."

Malcolm laughed and gave Ian the middle finger.

Andrea laughed, too. "I am so happy to have everyone here. This is the best. You know what, Ian? It just about killed Dad when you shut him out. He won't admit it, but he's probably in that bathroom crying his eyes out."

"Yeah," Ian said as he felt his own eyes get a little watery. "I don't know what I was thinking. I couldn't get that night out of my head and I blamed... Well, there is nothing I can do about it. It's time to move on."

"So true. Now that you are back, I need a favor," Andrea said as the smile on her face disappeared and was replaced by a worried look.

"What?"

"I need for you to talk to your nephew. He's about lost his everlasting mind. Wants to be a thug. For what? I don't know. I have taken him to tour the jails, sent him to etiquette classes, put him on punishment until he was blue in the face, but nothing seems to work. I sent him to live with his father, but..."

"Wait a minute. What do you mean you sent him to live with his father? When did you guys split up?" Ian asked.

"About two years ago," Andrea said, shaking her head.

"Damn," Ian said. "Are you for real?"

"Yes, Ian. Life went on while you stopped living. But anyway, that sorry thing sent him right back to me. Talking about how he won't listen to him. Duh! That's why I sent him to live with you in the first place, nut. Anyway, if you will talk to him before you leave, I would greatly appreciate it."

"What happened with you and Kenny—if you don't mind me asking?"

"No, I don't mind at all. I caught him having an affair with a man. And that man happened to be my boss. So I got fired, I sued his tail, settled out of court for a nice sum of money and now they are living in Florida."

"Are you serious?" Ian said. "Wow!"

"I wish I was lying," Andrea said as she shook her head. Ian saw that it all still pained her.

"This *is* Atlanta," Malcolm chimed in. "That's why I moved. I got tired of dudes looking at me crazy. I was at the movies one day and got a li'l teary eyed over a scene and this big buff dude gonna hand me a tissue and touched my leg talking 'bout he understands. I was like, 'hell nah.' Packed my bags that night and moved. Damn that."

"Shut up, Malcolm," Ian said.

"I'm just saying. I don't get down like that," Malcolm said.

"Are you okay, Andrea?" Ian asked.

"I don't have a choice. He claimed he couldn't live a lie anymore. So I guess he and his new man are over there living the truth. And I know KJ's behavior is a direct result of that."

"How old is KJ now?"

"He's thirteen."

"That's a tough age anyway without having to deal with the fact that you found out that your dad is gay. Where is he?" Ian asked.

"At a friend's house playing Xbox. That's where he spends most of his time. He's also suspended from school for having marijuana in his locker. Then he had the audacity to kick the drug dog," Andrea said.

"Damn," Ian said. "I'll be sure to talk to him, but he's not on vacation, so why are you letting him play videogames?"

"I can't monitor that boy twenty-four seven, so if he's gonna sneak and play it when I'm not home, I might as well not even fool myself," Andrea said.

Ian took a deep breath and nodded his head. He didn't realize how much he had dropped the ball on his responsibility to his family.

Colin walked out of the bathroom and motioned for Ian to come and join him on the deck.

"Granddaddy," Christian said, holding up his car as a sign that he was ready to play.

"Let me talk to your dad for a second and I will be all yours, okay? But in the meantime, why don't you show your Uncle Malcolm what you have," Colin said.

"Okay," Christian said.

"Whatcha got there, fireman?" Malcolm said, walking over to his nephew.

Ian and his father walked out on the spacious deck and enjoyed the view of a large, man-made lake equipped with a water fountain in the middle of it. About twenty-five ducks were swimming and every few minutes a fish would splash in the water. Colin lit up a Cuban cigar and offered one to his son. Ian declined.

"I'm happy to see you, son," Colin said as he took a pull on the cigar. "You seem like you're getting back to your old self. Joking with your old man, smiling and stuff."

"Yeah," Ian said, nodding his head. "I'm glad Andrea invited me over. It feels so good to be around family again. It's time to move on. I don't know what took me so long."

"We all have our own process, son," Colin said. "Trust me on that one. I still...well, anyway, I'm just happy that you seem to be happy, and that's all that matters."

"You're looking good, Pops. I see you've been taking care of yourself."

"Thanks. The doctor took me off of that pork. Hurt my feelings something awful too, son. I swear I almost cried like Malcolm. Ohh, what I wouldn't give for two smothered pork chops, a side of collard greens cooked with a big piece of fatback and some macaroni with cheese." Colin closed his eyes and appeared to savor the taste of what was now a forbidden meal.

Ian chuckled. "You don't need it. Soul food is too high in sodium and cholesterol. That's why black people are always dying off so early."

"Yeah, but everything they allow me to eat tastes like shit," Colin said, shaking his head. "The man even took ice cream from me. How can ice cream be bad for you? I drew the line right there. I eat it anyway. Rocky Road with the marshmallows in it or butter pecan. My God. I figure if I'm gonna die, then I'll be happy. I hope they find me with a half-gallon of butter pecan in my stomach."

Ian laughed. He didn't realize how much he missed his father's sense of humor.

"Man, you're crazy," Ian said.

"Yeah," Colin said, taking a drag from his Cuban cigar.

"Dad," Ian said, "I saw something on the news about that lady I helped out. I think she's in jail."

"Jail?"

"Yeah," Ian said. "They said something about her murdering her mother, but something about that story doesn't seem possible. At least not the way they described it. The newscaster said the mother was stabbed to death, but I can't see that. The woman I dropped off could barely walk."

Colin scratched his temple, a true sign he was in deep thought, and then nodded his head. "Why are you so interested in helping this woman? Didn't you tell me that you didn't know her?"

"I don't know her," Ian said. "I never met her before the day that I helped her, but something has me wanting to make sure she's okay. And it's going to eat me up until I find out what's going on."

"Yeah," Colin said. "I understand that. That's a DeMarco trait. Sometimes we can't leave well enough alone. I sent a couple of guys over to her place to snoop around. The guy who beat her up isn't dead."

"Yeah, I know," Ian said. "I saw him. I was on my route and he came running out of his house with his trash. Didn't seem to recognize me at all. No cuts, no bruises or anything from where I hit him. I saw his face split open with my own two eyes. There was blood all over the place and now nothing? I don't understand that one. I kept his trash and went through it. There were all kinds of dried-up bloody bandages in there but his face didn't show any signs of that beatdown."

"You said he was running?" Colin asked.

"Yep. He flagged us down because we had already passed his house."

"That's interesting. I need to have a conversation with the guys I sent over there. I was told that his legs were broken. Are you sure it was the same guy?"

"I'm one-hundred percent sure," Ian said.

"Okay," Colin said, calm as ever. "I'll look into it."

"Thanks. Did Andrea talk to you about KJ?" Ian asked.

"Nah," he said. "But I kind of figured something was going on with him. He's a teenager and she's now a single mother. Sometimes that can be a recipe for disaster. What did she tell you?"

"She said he's lost his mind. Doing some crazy things. Got caught with some weed at school and has been acting out."

Colin frowned. "Well, you talk to him and keep me posted. It's got to be tough in today's society when your daddy turns gay on you, but it's amplified when that dummy gets on television and talks about how gays should be allowed to get married."

"He was on TV?" Ian asked. "I would've never suspected Kenny to be gay."

"He's one of them down-low males. Or at least, he was. I have more respect for the ones who walk around switching than for them closet punks. That's why the disease rate is so high. Sleeping with a man but then wanna run around and jump in bed with a woman because they are too weak to be who they are. If you gay, then just be gay. You don't have to walk around wearing dresses, but don't lie to people or yourself."

"Yeah," Ian said, nodding his head in agreement. "What television show was he on?"

"I don't know. I can't keep up with that stuff. He didn't think about his son and how his coming out would affect him. But this is a different day, son," Colin said.

Ian looked out as the daylight turned to dusk and noticed that the ducks had gone on their way.

"Dinner's ready, guys," Andrea's voice said, but she was nowhere to be seen.

"Oh, she can't come out here and tell us; she has to show off the intercom, huh?" Ian said with a smile. "This place is off the chain."

"Yeah. It's nice, and I'm starving," Colin said. "Let's go eat."

R avon hadn't been out of prison for a full week and yet he was already on the run. He wasn't sure where he was going, but he had to leave. He rushed around his girlfriend's apartment, throwing all of his clothes and belongings into a big Hefty trash looking for any and everything he might need for his new life far away from the state of Georgia. Sweat was pouring from his pores, even though the temperature outside was below thirty. He paused and calmed himself. He looked at his woman who was sitting on the sofa rocking back and forth. Lisa was a very pretty woman. She was naturally large and she wore it well. Her cream-colored skin was flushed from crying. They had waited five long years to be together and now they were about to be separated again.

"I didn't know what else to do!" Ravon said after he shared every single detail of what had happened at his mother's house and how he wished he had never taken the phone call. "I didn't have a choice. It was him or me. I really didn't have a choice."

"I know, so why don't you call the police and tell them what happened?" Lisa pleaded through the stream of tears running down her chubby cheeks.

"Lisa, I can't do that. They will lock me up first, then ask questions later. I just left prison. I'm guilty until proven innocent in their eyes."

"But the key word is that you're innocent. So let them prove you innocent. I have some money saved. We can get a lawyer," she said.

"Even if they find me innocent, I still had a gun. They will try to send me back to prison for that alone. I can't take that chance," Ravon said.

"I knew you shouldn't have gone over there. I could feel that something wasn't right," Lisa said.

"Yeah, I had that feeling, too," Ravon said, shaking his head in disbelief at the situation he found himself in. "I should've stayed my ass right here. I can't go back to prison, Lisa. I can't even take the chance."

"Where are you going?" she asked.

"I don't know," Ravon said. "I can't believe this is happening to me. I must be cursed or something. Damn."

"No, you're not cursed. I am. I finally find a man who treats me good and this happens. I wanna go with you, Ray."

"If things cool down, I'll send for you," Ravon said. "I hope that nosey-ass lady next door didn't see me."

Ravon walked over to his woman. He hugged her as tight as he could before pulling himself away.

"Is your car going to make it on the highway?" Lisa asked, referring to the hooptie he had just purchased.

"We'll see," he said and gave her one last kiss before walking toward the front door.

"Ray, wait," Lisa said, nervously rubbing her hands together. "How am I going to get in touch with you?"

"I don't know. I'll get my hands on another cell phone and call you."

"No," she said and ran to the bedroom and returned with her cell phone. "Take this. I'll get a new one tomorrow. I need to be able to reach you."

"A'ight, thanks," he said.

"I love you, Ray."

"I love you, too," he said and reached out to wipe away her tears.

"I wish you could stay!" she said, stalling for more time.

"Me too, but listen, if the police come by here, you tell them I've been out of town looking for work for a few days."

"Okay," she said.

He turned around and gave her one more look. He placed his hand to his mouth and blew her a kiss before walking out of the apartment. He hustled down the stairs with his belongings slung across his shoulders. Before walking into the parking lot, he scanned the area for police, and once the coast was clear, he ran over to his jalopy and got in. He turned the ignition and the hooptie came to life. He couldn't help but relive how peaceful his life had been just a few short hours ago.

Ravon lay on his back smoking a Philly Blunt cigar with the tobacco replaced with a different herb of marijuana that had a purplish hue. This potent weed was imported from the streets of Los Angeles and was known there as the "sticky icky." He had always loved the way weed smoke made him feel. His troubles were a thing of the past as long as he had some weed in his system, and as he inhaled "sticky icky" into his lungs, the world was a beautiful place.

Lisa, his girlfriend, was lying beside him, totally unconscious and snoring for the entire neighborhood to hear. Sleep always stole her away after their sex sessions. He looked at her and smiled as if his penis was the reason she was totally exhausted. "Yeah," he said. "Don't go to war with the big dog, girl. Look at cha. Knocked the hell out," he said as he took another puff.

Ravon and Lisa shared a small two-bedroom apartment in a

middle-class neighborhood in Stone Mountain with her son, Devin. Devin was away for the weekend with his father, so they had the apartment all to themselves.

Ravon took a deep pull from the blunt and held it in his lungs until he coughed. He couldn't understand how something that felt so good could cause such violent convulsions within his body. With every puff, he felt as if he was about to lose a lung. He threw his legs over the edge of the bed, stood up, and stretched. His head was a little woozy from the weed, but his stomach was begging to be fed. He walked into the kitchen, reached into the cabinet, grabbed a box of Frosted Flakes and a big Tupperware container, and emptied half the box of cereal into the bowl. He opened the refrigerator, pulled out a gallon of milk, and covered the flakes. A big smile creased his face when he thought about all of those nights in jail when he wished he could do something as simple as get up and walk into another room. Now he was free and he couldn't help but savor the moment. He put the milk and the cereal box back in their places, grabbed his bowl and opened the sliding door to the balcony. He walked outside and took in the night air. If someone would have walked by at that moment, they would have thought he was out of his mind. Here he was, sitting on the balcony at two in the morning, in the winter, wearing nothing but his birthday suit, and eating a bowl of cereal. If prison taught him anything, it was to never take life for granted. He promised himself that once he was free, he would enjoy the little things. Things like taking a walk in the park. People who lived in the hood never took advantage of nature. He had been living in Atlanta all of his life and never once visited the King Center, Stone Mountain Park, Sweet Auburn Avenue, Ebenezer Baptist Church or any of the other historical places the city had to offer. He had spent his entire life confined to a small area of the city all because he never opened himself up to think outside of his comfort zone. But that was all about to change.

The apartment phone rang and he jumped to get it before it woke Lisa up. He placed his bowl on the counter and answered the phone.

"Hello," he said, wondering who could be calling the house this time of morning.

"Ravon," Sara said. "This ya momma."

"I know."

"Well, I need for you to get over here now. These li'l bad ass kids out there selling drugs on my front porch. Now I know they dumb but I didn't know the li'l fuckers were crazy. I told them I was gonna call the police and they ran off, but now they're back. I went outside with my gun and all they did was showed me theirs. I'm tired of these li'l bastards. They making all kind of noise and I can't get no damn sleep."

"Call the police," he said.

"And play that li'l game all night? The police are full of shit. I ain't fooling with them. You coming or not?"

Ravon sighed. He was really enjoying his high and really didn't feel like dealing with his mother or the brats who were giving her problems but he promised himself while sitting in prison that he would look after the woman.

"Hello," Sara said.

"Yeah, I'm here. I'll be over there in a minute."

"You better hurry up because my patience is running out. I don't wanna have to shoot one of these li'l niggas."

"Don't do that," Ravon said, stomping his foot with frustration. "I'm on my way."

"Yeah, well… Where is your cell phone? I've been calling you for two days. Good thing I remembered that I wrote Lisa's number down on the calendar."

"I lost it."

"Lost it? Damn, boy, you would forget your head if it wasn't attached to your neck."

"Have you talked to Zola?"

"Hell no. For what?"

"'Cause that's your daughter."

"No, she ain't no daughter of mine. I can do without her ass. She's still running around here feeling sorry for herself and blaming me for everything that's wrong in her life."

"And so you're just going to...well, whatever," Ravon said, deciding against trying to salvage a relationship that was forever broken.

"How did you lose your damn phone?"

"You want me to come over or are you gonna keep asking me questions?" Ravon asked.

Something cracked in his ear as his mother slammed her end of the phone down as if that should be a good enough answer. He shook his head at the nutcase he had for a mother and placed the phone back on its base. After grabbing his bowl of cereal, he walked into the living room and sat on the sofa to finish feeding his munchies. Ravon grabbed the remote control and flipped through the channels. The video channels were all filled with infomercials, so he flipped through the rotation again.

"Seven hundred channels and not a damn thing worth watching," he said to himself. "Damn, I wish I wouldn't have answered that phone. Just my luck I get over there and have to shoot one of those li'l fools."

History told him that any confrontation with youngsters this time of morning could easily turn violent. And that could lead him right back to prison or dead. He picked up the phone and dialed 9-1-1.

"Nine-one-one. What is your emergency?"

"I'd like to report a trespassing at my mother's house," Ravon said.

"Hold, please," the operator said.

Ravon frowned but held the line. After being in that same position for four minutes, he pulled the phone away from his ear and looked at it. "Hello? Damn. Nine-one-one is a joke. What kind of emergency line is this?"

After hanging up on 9-1-1, Ravon stood and wondered why he was going to go over to Sara's house to check on her. He didn't really care about her, because she wouldn't allow you to care about her. But she was still his mother. Something inside of him was telling him to stay away, but he brushed the thought away, walked back into the bedroom and got dressed. He put on some underwear, a pair of Levi jeans, and a sweatshirt and slipped his size twelve feet into his trusty Timberland boots. He grabbed the car keys and leaned down and kissed Lisa on her forehead. He stood and stared at his woman. Physically, she wasn't his type but she was good as gold. And the way she stood by him when he was incarcerated placed her at the top of his list. Lisa was a few pounds overweight, her skin was almost white, and she was as ghetto as the next chick. The thing that separated Lisa from the other hood girls was that she wanted a better life for herself and her son. And even more important, she was willing to put in the work to get there. She had enrolled in night classes to earn her Associate's Degree from Georgia Perimeter College and was trying to get Ravon to do the same. His superficial side hated to admit it, but he loved her.

Lisa stirred and looked at him with sleepy eyes. "Where are you going, Ray?"

"I need to run by Sara's house. Some kids are out there bothering her and I need to go talk to them. I called the police but those bastards put me on hold and never came back to the phone."

"Oh, okay," she said and rolled back over. "Be careful."

"Will do," he said, grabbing his coat and the keys for her car. He had just purchased a little Saturn for himself but it was in dire need a muffler. Whenever he drove it, everyone within a five-mile radius could hear him coming.

Ravon got into Lisa's Honda and headed toward his mother's house, which was only about a ten-minute drive from where he was. He backed out of the parking lot and had this sinking feeling in his gut. Something wasn't right. He made a few turns here and there, and before long he was turning onto the street where his mother lived.

Ravon drove slowly as he scanned the streets looking for signs of trouble. As he eased past Sara's house, he checked out the front porch but didn't see any kids. He drove down to the end of the street, then turned around in someone's driveway. Coming back up the street, he slowly pulled into an empty spot in front of Sara's house. He stared at the house before he got out of the car, then walked up the driveway and stopped. Was he imagining that he saw the curtain in the living room open and then close?

Ravon's gut was screaming at him to get out of there, so he turned around and went to the car. He opened the driver side door, leaned inside and felt up under the seat until his fingers touched the cold steel of his .38-caliber handgun. He gripped it, slipped it in his pocket and flipped the car door shut. Then he turned back around, walked up the driveway, and climbed the stairs to the old white house.

He knocked on the door but nobody answered. He knocked harder, but there was only silence on the other side. He scratched his head and walked over to see if he could see inside the house. The television was on and he thought he saw Sara lying on the sofa. He knocked on the window but she didn't move. Did he just see somebody's shadow in the kitchen area? He pulled his gun out and jumped off of the porch. Something wasn't right and he could feel it as he made his way around the side of the house to the back door. Ravon eased up the back steps and tried the door knob. He turned the handle and much to his surprise, it opened. His heart was racing so fast that he thought a cardiac arrest was on the horizon. His pistol was already in his hand so he chambered a round and held his gun in front of him. As he stepped inside of the kitchen, his instincts kicked in just in time… "POW!" a gunshot blasted into the door behind him, sending wood fragments and splinters everywhere.

Ravon jumped down onto the floor, stuck his gun around the wall and let off two shots from his own gun. He only had six bullets so he made sure to keep that in mind. He stayed low and waited for whoever it was to return fire. He heard a man groan and make a sound he'd never heard before. Down on his stomach, he crawled very slowly, almost snail-like, until he could see in the direction where he sent his bullets. He looked to his right and saw the bottom of two black boots. A white man was lying down on the floor clutching his chest.

"Pow!" Ravon's gunshot blast shook the calm of the night as he shot the man one more time. He wasn't sure if he was dead or if he was trying to lure him in. The white man's body shook and he grabbed his shoulder with his left hand, but he didn't take his right one from his chest. Ravon jumped up after seeing the man wasn't a threat anymore and walked over to him.

"Who the hell are you?" he asked the man who was now bleeding from his mouth, chest and shoulder.

The man didn't respond. He couldn't respond if he wanted to. His eyes were fluttering and his mouth was opening and closing as he gasped through the flowing blood for air.

Ravon looked at him and could tell right away that the man

had done prison time. Tattoos were all over the place, even on his face and neck. His long, stringy hair was pulled back into a ponytail.

Ravon looked down and saw that the man's gun was a few feet away from him. He thought about picking it up, but didn't want his fingerprints on it, so he kicked it over to where he was standing. He took a few steps toward the living room and could see his mother. Sara was covered in blood and not moving. He called her name as he eased over to her. As he got closer, he could see her eyes were wide open but without life. Ravon looked around and decided it was time to get out of the house. He was a convicted felon who had just shot a man, a white man at that. In the state of Georgia, that was enough to get you death by lethal injection. Never mind the fact that this man was in his mother's house, that she was dead and had taken a shot at him. None of that would matter in a court of law.

Ravon took a deep breath and hustled back through the kitchen. He glanced over at the man he had just shot and noticed him grimacing in pain and holding onto his wounds. His mouth was wide open as he gasped for air, but it was a losing battle. In one last move of desperation, the man looked up at Ravon with pleading eyes. "Help," he managed to say.

Ravon did a double-take and was amazed at the man's arrogance. *You just killed my mother, tried to kill me and yet you think I'm going to help you stay alive?*

There would be no help coming. The white man had seen his black face and that was bad news. He wasn't going back to prison for anybody, especially for this murderous bastard lying in his own blood on his mother's kitchen floor. Ravon turned his gun on the man and fired another shot into his heaving chest. All of a sudden, the eyes lost all signs of life and his midsection stopped moving. There was a weird gargling sound, then a dark substance flowed from the dead man's mouth, and he closed his eyes for good.

Ravon ran back into the house with his gun out in front of him, checking all of the bedrooms and making sure that nobody else was in there. Once he knew he was alone, he ran from the house through the back door. He hustled to the Honda and jumped inside. His heart was racing and he sat still, trying to calm himself before turning on the ignition. He looked back at his mother's house and shook his head. Two people were in there and both of them were dead. He eased away from his mother's house, being careful not to speed.

14

Zola stared at the television set that was mounted on the wall near the window of her hospital room. She couldn't believe what she was seeing. Her picture was being plastered all over the evening news as a prime suspect in the death of her mother. God knew that she hated Sara with every ounce of her being, but she could never kill her. It wasn't in her nature. She thought about the many times when she almost fell down while jogging to avoid stepping on an ant or some other insect; now she was being plastered on Fox 5 News as a lead suspect in the murder of a real live person.

There was a knock on the door and Zola pulled her nightgown up a little closer to her neck.

"Come in," she said.

Kecia walked in, followed by a woman with closely cropped hair and a very light complexion. The woman had a pleasant smile and looked very familiar to her.

"Hi there," Kecia said with a wide smile as if she had hit the lottery or something. "I really hate to show up like this with a visitor, but whatever."

"How did you guys get in? Visiting hours are over," Zola asked.

"Girl, please. I'm from New York," Kecia said. "I told them I was your family and I came all the way from California and that I have a plane to catch in the morning."

"You're a mess, but you are family," Zola said. "The only sister I have."

"That's right," Kecia said. "Anyway, this is my godmother, Pearl. Pearl Cleage."

"Hi." Zola smiled as she connected the name with the face. She had read one of Ms. Cleage's books a few months ago when she heard about how good it was on Oprah Winfrey's website. "I love your work."

"Thank you," Pearl said with a soothing, velvety-like voice. "I hope you don't mind me showing up like this."

"Oh, no. Not at all," Zola said. "I'm a huge fan. It's a pleasure to meet you."

Pearl smiled and nodded her appreciation. "I understand you're in a bit of a bind. I want to help."

"Being in a bind is the story of my life, Mrs. Cleage," Zola said. "I have no idea how I'm the so-called prime suspect because I had nothing to do with killing my mother."

"They are just sweating you," Kecia said. "Fishing for anything they can use against you."

"If that's the case, then why is my picture on television?" Zola asked. "When I left her house, she was sitting on the sofa watching television."

"I hear that you and your mother weren't close?" Pearl asked.

"No. I didn't like her and she didn't like me," Zola said.

Pearl frowned and shook her head as if she was thinking this was a story she had heard too many times before. Then she walked closer to the bed and ran her hand across Zola's face, smoothing her hair back into place.

"It has to be illegal for them to do that to me, right? I wish I could afford an attorney to sue them," Zola said, fighting a losing battle with her tears. She had had to be strong for so long, but there was something about being in the room with these two women that made her let down her guard. There was something special, almost angelic, about the lady standing over her. Pearl's eyes and soft touch told Zola that she could let go of all the pain, frustration and pent-up rage because now there was a soft place to land. In less than five minutes of knowing the woman, she trusted her with everything she had.

What was that all about? she wondered.

"It's okay," Pearl said, embracing Zola's hand with both of hers and seemingly reading her mind. "We will get through this together. I know it's hard, but you are not alone."

"Pearl has a friend who is a very good attorney and she is already downtown talking to the powers that be on your behalf," Kecia said.

"That's right," Pearl said, shaking her head. "Your picture won't be shown anymore."

"I called her the minute I left," Kecia said. "I didn't like the look on those detectives' faces. I've been interning downtown with the public defender's office and I'm well aware of how they do things. It's a shame how much pressure these detectives are under to clear the books. But we're not going to let them frame you. I hope you don't mind, but I told Pearl everything that you told me about your past."

Zola nodded her head, but didn't respond.

"The attorney's name is Sharon Capers and she's very good. One of the best in the business," Pearl said.

"I don't have the money right now," Zola said. "I can get it, but I will have to move a few things around. I have a three hundred thousand dollar loft and a hundred thousand dollar car but no liquid cash. I will sell whatever…"

"No, ma'am," Pearl said, shaking her head and cutting her off. "This is not about money. The only thing I want is for you to get better. And once this is all behind you, you'll help someone else. Pretty simple, huh?"

Zola nodded her head. "I don't know what to say."

"There is nothing that needs to be said," Pearl said. "But listen, I really need to get home. My husband and I are going on a little vacation in the morning, but you are in very capable hands. I will be checking on you, okay?"

"Okay," Zola said. "I hope you have fun on your trip."

"Thank you," Pearl said, leaning down and kissing Zola on her forehead. "You get yourself back strong and healthy, and once you are out of here, I would love to have you over for dinner."

"I would love that," Zola said, nodding her head. "Thank you so much for everything."

"Don't mention it," Pearl said. "Kecia, I'll see you later, girl."

Kecia smiled and walked over to Pearl. She gave her a tight hug and the two shared a long embrace. Pearl turned and smiled at Zola one last time before walking out of the door.

Kecia walked over and sat down beside Zola. "You know your place is so comfortable. I appreciate you letting me stay there."

"No problem," Zola said. "It's the least I could do. Thank you so much for getting this attorney for me."

Kecia fanned her off.

Zola couldn't stop the tears from running down her face. All of her childhood she had wanted a sister and a real mom, and that had eluded her. Now she wasn't sure how to take all of this love she was receiving from Pearl, a complete stranger, and Kecia, who, before this tragedy, was an associate at best. The mere fact that these women had already set the wheels in motion to get the police off of her back placed them on the top of her list of dear friends. There was another knock on the door and in walked a tall, white man who was a dead ringer for an older Brad Pitt.

Chad Benjamin walked in a few seconds after Pearl walked out. He nodded at the two ladies as he entered the room. Kecia paused and asked Zola with her eyes if the man was a friend or foe.

Zola nodded that he was okay.

"Hi there," Chad said to Zola.

"Hi, Chad," Zola said, looking behind him. "How are you? Where is Jason?"

Chad didn't respond.

"Is everything okay?" Zola said, assuming the look on his face was bad news about her son.

"Yes. Everything is fine. Jason is doing great," Chad said.

"Kecia," Zola said. "This is Chad Benjamin. He's my son's..." she said, not sure what to call the man.

"Nice to meet you, Chad," Kecia said, reaching out her hand.

"It's nice to meet you, too," Chad said with a pleasant smile as he shook Kecia's hand.

"Well, I'll let you guys talk," Kecia said. "Zola, I'll be back to check up on you a little later on. If not tonight, then tomorrow for sure. I put my number on the pad by the phone, so call me if you need anything. I love you, girl."

"I love you, too. Be careful out there," Zola said and waited for Kecia to leave.

"I will. Bye. Bye, Chad. It was nice meeting you," Kecia said as she hustled out of the door.

Chad nodded to her and looked down at Zola with a concerned expression on his face.

"Have a seat," Zola said as she pointed at the chair by the window. "What's up?"

"What's going on with you, Zola? Do you need anything?"

"What do you mean?"

"I was watching the news and..."

"I didn't have anything to do with that," Zola said. "That was my mother and we weren't the best of friends, but I would never do what those people are saying."

"I believe you, but the problem is… Well, I won't beat around the bush. Jason saw it and he's quite upset."

"What?" Zola said as her heart hit the floor.

"I tried to keep him away from it and I did for the six o'clock news, but somehow my wife found a way to let him see it on the seven o'clock broadcast. He's torn up about it."

Zola's tears came back. "Oh my God!" she cried. "I'm totally innocent. I don't want Jason thinking his mother is some crazy murderer. I didn't do anything."

Chad stood and walked over to her. He reached out and touched her hand and gave it a comforting squeeze. "I believe you," he said. "Have you gotten an attorney?"

"Why did she let him see that?" Zola said, feeling her anger rise. She could strangle that woman for trying to poison her son's mind with those shady police officers' lies.

"I don't know, but you can best believe that it caused a huge argument. I'm not sure what her motivation was behind that, but she was wrong," Chad said. "I'm sorry that it happened."

"I wanna talk to Jason," Zola said.

Chad whipped out his cell phone and pushed a button.

"Where is Jason?" he said, not bothering with a greeting. "Well, wake him up! Never mind where I am; just go and get Jason. Carmen, I'm not getting into this with you. Now will you go and get Jason or should I come home and get him myself?"

Chad sat down and looked at the floor while he waited. He frowned after being placed on hold for a little too long. "This woman," he said, shaking his head.

Zola's heart ached at the thought of her child seeing her picture being attached to the word "murder." Her son's opinion of her was the most important thing in the world. Over the last year she had been privately planning a strategy to get Jason back under her care but now there was a sense of urgency like never before. She liked Chad and she used to like his wife; at least she did until Carmen decided to poison her son's mind against her. Now she knew it was time he came home. The Benjamins had taken care of Jason when she couldn't and she appreciated that. They had exposed him to people, places and cultures that she could only dream about, but they couldn't love him like she could. And now this latest stunt by Carmen was even more motivation to get her life together and prove to the world that she was somebody.

"She hung up," Chad said, taking the phone away from his ear and looking at the screen saver. "I can't believe she hung up. What is wrong with that woman?"

"Don't worry about it," Zola said with a steely determination. "I'll take care of it."

"I just wanted to make sure you were okay," he said as he stood up. "I will have Jason call you once I get home. Keep your cell phone on."

"He'll have to call the room. I don't have my cell phone with me. I'm not supposed to use it in here."

"Will do," Chad said walking over and getting the number from the phone on the nightstand.

Ian looked at his watch. It was almost one o'clock in the morning. Christian was fast asleep on the sofa. His father had already left and he and Malcolm were sitting on the deck enjoying the night. They lit the fire to keep warm and played catch up. Ian filled him in with how stagnant his life had been since he had lost his wife and daughter and Malcolm filled him in on his life out west.

"I guess I need to get out of here, man," Ian said as he removed his feet off of the patio ottoman. "I'm enjoying the scene too much. Gotta get back to the ghetto."

"There were too many sacrifices made for you to be living in the ghetto," Malcolm said. "I don't want my nephew caught up in some hood crossfire. Then I'm really gonna cry."

"Yeah," Ian said as he turned down the heat on the fire pit. "I'm way ahead of ya, li'l bro. That's been on my mind heavy lately. Before we came over here, the natives were outside shooting."

"Come on, Ian," Malcolm said. "If not for yourself, do it for Christian."

Ian nodded. "So, when are you headed back to the west coast?"

"I need to be back on Monday morning. I'm starting a new job at the University of Washington as a career counselor. We fly out Sunday night. I love flying at night, man."

"Oh, yeah? You have a lovely family, bro. I'm proud of you. Got you an Asian woman, huh? She's a gem. I like her."

"Yeah, man. She plays that Asian shit, but her ass was raised in Tacoma and she got some ghetto ways. Her Kool-Aid's sweeter than a mother. I think she puts about three cups of sugar in a gallon, bro. And will she cuss. Oh Lord. She gets mad and starts mixing that Asian and hood talk together so much. It's bad, bro. 'You mudda-fucka-ass-licky-stupid-dick-bastard,'" Malcolm said with a chuckle. "You don't believe me? I'mma piss her off before we leave so you can hear how she acts."

"Man," Ian said, laughing. "You're crazy. Leave Ming alone."

"You better leave Ming alone. She needs to leave me alone. You know I can't beat her, right? Hell, I met her in a Karate class. She was my instructor. But you know what I told her, you gotta sleep sometime," Malcolm said with a straight face.

"Man. I am not messing with you. You are a complete nut," Ian said as he placed the top on the fire pit. "I gotta get this boy up so we can get out of here."

"Ian, let him spend the night," Malcolm pleaded. "I wanna spend some time with him. Maybe I can take him to the arcade or something in the morning. He's been asking everybody if he could spend the night. The boy is tired of yo' ass."

Ian chuckled. "Let me talk to Andrea."

"Whatchu think she gonna say, no?"

"Just being courteous, man," Ian said.

Andrea was sitting in a chair across from the fireplace, watching television. "Y'all finally decided to come in the house?" she asked.

"Yeah," Ian said. "It's about time we get out of here."

"We?" Malcolm said. "How about you just take your butt on and leave my nephew here."

"Yeah, Ian. He wants to stay," Andrea said. "Let him sleep."

Ian walked over to Christian who was snoring on the sofa. Ian gave his son a gentle nudge to wake him and Christian looked up.

"Hi, Daddy," he said. sitting up and rubbing his eyes. "Can I spend the night?"

Ian sighed. "I guess so," he said.

Christian smiled, but he was too tired to do much of anything else, so he lay his head back down on the sofa and drifted back off to sleep.

This would be the first time Ian had ever spent a night without his child, but it wasn't fair to keep treading down the path he had been on. Christian didn't just belong to him; he belonged to his entire family.

The side door leading to the garage opened and KJ walked in. "What's up, Uncle Malcolm?" he said in his deep teenage voice.

"What's up?" Malcolm said, looking at his watch. "That damn sun gonna be up in a minute. Where you been?"

"Next door," KJ said, then turned his attention to Ian. "Ohhhh, snap. What's up, Uncle Ian? I haven't seen you in ages."

"How you doing, KJ?" Ian said walking over to give his almost six feet tall nephew a frat brother hug. "I can't believe how big you've gotten. Are you playing sports?"

"Football and baseball," KJ said.

"When he's not suspended from school," Andrea said.

"Aww, Mom," KJ complained with a frown. "I haven't seen Uncle Ian in I don't know how long and you gotta start fussing. Don't nobody wanna hear all that."

KJ was the spitting image of his father with a little dose of Andrea thrown in around the lips and cheeks. He was as dark as a Hershey bar and had a head full of hair twisted up into little dreadlocks.

"I'm glad I waited around or I would've missed you," Ian said.

"Yeah," KJ said. "I was just two doors down at my friend's house.

Is that Christian over there?" he asked, walking over to his little cousin.

"Yep," Ian said. "That's him."

"Boy, he's getting big," KJ said.

"Yeah," Ian said. "And so are you. How tall are you?"

"I don't know," KJ said. "Five-eleven, maybe six feet. Something like that."

"I'm going to bed," Malcolm said. He reached out to Ian and gave him his fifteenth hug of the night; then he turned to KJ and punched him in the chest. "Whatcha gone do? Huh, buck up? I'll knock the taste outta ya mouth."

KJ grabbed the spot where he was hit and smiled. "Uncle Malcolm is crazy."

Even after all that he had heard about his nephew, Ian couldn't help but be proud of the young man he was looking at. That was until he took a closer look at KJ's eyes.

"Are you about to leave?" KJ asked.

"Yeah, man," Ian said, zeroing in on the bloodshot eyes that were a sure sign of drugs. "I've been here for hours. I called your cell. Why didn't you answer your phone?"

"It's dead. I forgot to charge the thing last night."

"Is that right? Well, listen to me, nephew. I need a favor, KJ."

"Sure," he said. "Anything for you, Uncle Ian."

"I need for you to help me move some things at my house. Why don't you grab a change of clothes and ride with me."

KJ paused.

Ian could see that the boy knew something was up.

"I can ask my mom to bring me over in the morning. I'm a little tired," KJ said in a futile attempt to stay home and out of his uncle's tough glare.

Andrea cut in, "I'll tell you right now the answer is no. You can go right now while you have a ride. And you can stay over there for all I care."

KJ dropped his head.

Andrea leaned down and picked Christian up. "Ian, call me tomorrow. If you need for me to pack up all of his stuff, just say the word."

"Andrea," Ian said, shaking his head. "Don't do that."

"I'm fed up with this boy," Andrea said. "I swear I am. He's been screwing up time after time, and I'm tired of it."

"Well, you can be fed up, but keep it to yourself," Ian said.

"See how she is? Always putting me down. If you don't want me here, then I'll leave," KJ said.

"And go where?" Andrea said. "Your daddy doesn't want you. He's with who he wants to be with; a damn man."

"Andrea!" Ian snapped at his sister. "What's wrong with you? Have you lost your mind? Why would you say something like that?"

"Because it's the damn truth. And every time I get on his case for being a screw up, he claim he's going to leave. Well, leave, KJ. I don't give a damn. As a matter of fact, I would welcome it. Get out."

"Are you the parent or the child?!" Ian snapped.

"Whatever. He can go live with his faggot-ass father," Andrea said as she huffed and puffed. After adjusting Christian on her hip, she walked out of the living room toward her bedroom.

"Uncle Ian," KJ said, dropping his head in shame. His shoulders slumped and it was clear this situation with his father had all but defeated him.

Ian could tell that Andrea's words were all his nephew could take.

"Hey," Ian said as he placed both of his hands on KJ's shoulders.

"You don't have to own that. Don't you dare drop your head because of the actions of someone else. I don't care if it's your mother or your father. You are your own man and God made you perfect. If you ask me, your mother is dead wrong and she needs to grow up," Ian said loud enough for his sister to hear him.

"Can you give me a few minutes to get my stuff together? I can't stay here with her anymore. All she does is put me down and call me names. I'm not gay and every time she gets mad, which is all the time, she calls me some homosexual name."

Ian shook his head. He really hated that his sister was carrying on this way and he planned on having a long talk with her about it.

"I wanna get out of here," KJ said, not seeming to miss a beat from the times he used to share with his uncle when he was a small kid.

"I understand," Ian said, nodding his head. "Go ahead and get what you need. You can stay with me as long as you like."

"Thanks, Uncle Ian," KJ said as a rush of relief ran over his face. He turned and almost ran to his room to pack a bag.

Zola was feeling a little better. Her facial bruises were still visible, but the pain had subsided a great deal. Whatever medicine they were giving her was working miracles on her once-aching ribs. They were still sore, but the sharp pains had subsided a great deal. Her doctor had finally authorized her to be released and she couldn't have been happier.

Five days of drugs and the hard hospital bed had done their job, but she had had enough and was ready to get on with the business of getting her son back. Sharon Capers, her attorney, had called her and assured her that the police wouldn't be contacting her again. She was a no-nonsense type of woman and seemed to be just as sharp as Pearl and Kecia said she was. The mere fact that she had someone like Mrs. Capers on her team allowed her to rest easier and focus all of her attention on getting Jason back where he needed to be.

Zola looked out the window of the hospital's lobby at the sunny Atlanta day. There was a little boy who was crying as he lay on his father's lap. She couldn't help but wish that her son could also share a father and son bond.

Zola stood staring out the window at the busy Atlanta streets and thought back to when she felt all alone in this world. A smile eased on her face as she realized those feelings no longer existed. Kecia was on her way to pick her up and it felt good, knowing that she now had someone she could count on. Ever since this incident with Andre had happened, Kecia had become the little sister that she had always wanted but never had. Before she could get too deep into her thoughts, Zola's name was called and one of the nurses who treated her brought out a wheelchair.

"Hospital policy," the nurse said, hunching her shoulders.

"I understand," Zola said as she walked over and sat down in the chair. "As long as I'm leaving here and can get in my own bed, you can push me out on a gurney."

"I'm sure you're happy to leave," the nurse said while wheeling her down the hallway, then out to the parking area. "Good luck with everything."

"Thanks," Zola said.

"And I'm really sorry to hear about your mother," the nurse said. "I try to mind my business but when your sister came in and told me your mother had passed, well, I didn't mind breaking the visitation rules for that. Mothers are special and I'm really sorry to hear of your loss."

Zola nodded her head and pretended to be grieving, but she was thinking, *if you only knew my mother, you wouldn't be singing that tune.*

"Thanks. I appreciate your condolences," Zola said.

"My name is Mimi," the nurse said, extending her hand. "I didn't want to be all in your business while you were a patient—besides that's against hospital rules—but I lost my mother last year and well, let me just say, it's been tough."

"I'm sorry to hear that, Mimi," Zola said and couldn't help but envy whatever relationship the nurse had with her mother that would make her tear up at the mere mention of her death.

"Your sister is a very sharp young lady," Mimi said, pointing toward Kecia, who was running around the side of her Mini Cooper to open the passenger door.

"Yeah," Zola said with a smile. "I think I'll keep her around."

"I have a surprise for you," Kecia said, smiling from ear to ear. Before she could reach the passenger door, it opened on its own. Out stepped a little boy who was about four-feet-five tall and wearing khaki pants and a maroon polo shirt beneath a navy blue blazer with a gold crescent on the breast pocket. The little boy smiled and ran toward Zola.

"Jason!" Zola screamed so loud they could hear her inside the hospital.

"Hi, Mom," he said with a wide smile.

"Oh my God," Zola said as she jumped up out of the wheel-chair and ran to her son. She leaned down and hugged him so tight that her ribs started hurting again. "How are you? I missed you so much, little boy."

"I missed you, too," Jason said with his very proper diction. "I haven't seen you in months. Are you okay?"

"I'm doing fine," Zola said, reaching down and hugging him again. She turned to Kecia and asked, "What's Jason doing with you?"

"Ask him," she said with a blank expression on her face.

Zola's smile disappeared and she looked down at her son. "Jason?" she said.

Jason dropped his head. "I ran away," he said.

"You did what?" Zola said and all of a sudden, she looked around as if someone might be watching them.

"I ran away. Carmen is mean," he said. "She always talks bad about you. She's not nice, like she acts in front of you. She's a faker and I don't want to live with her anymore."

"Where did you get him from?" Zola asked Kecia.

"He called your cell phone. Here ya go," Kecia said, reaching out to give the BlackBerry back to Zola. "He said he was at the bus stop and well, I had to go get him. When I got there, he was standing there all alone. He's smart for his age but he's still only six years old, so I wasn't about to tell him to go back."

"Oh my goodness," Zola said. "Listen, Jason. You have to know better than to be out here all by yourself. Anything could've happened to you. That was very dangerous."

"But it didn't and I'm with you again," he said with a child's innocence.

Zola sighed and looked around again. Was someone playing a cruel joke on her?

"I'm not going back over there. I'll run away again," Jason said.

Zola sighed. "There's certain ways we have to do things, Jason. You can't just…. Never mind. Let's go."

Jason jumped into the back seat of Kecia's small, yet surprisingly spacious, car and Zola sat in the passenger seat. Once Kecia was behind the wheel, they buckled up and were headed out of the parking lot.

"I'm hungry," Kecia said. "Lunch is on me, if ya'll wanna eat."

"We have to get Mr. Man here back to school," Zola said, turning around in her seat and peering at her son.

"Nooo," Jason said. "I wanna stay with you. I'm only going to run away again. This time you won't know where I'll be."

"Jason," Zola said with a frown. The mere thought of her child out in this cruel world all alone sent a chill down her spine. "I want you to stay with me, too, but we have to do this the right way or I'll be in big trouble."

"Carmen said you're going to jail because you did something bad," Jason said as he stared straight into his mother's eyes.

"Listen to me, Jason. I haven't done anything to anybody. Chad told me that you saw the news, but that was all one big mistake.

I would never lie to you. You do know that, don't you?" Zola asked, staring into the little boy's eyes that mimicked her own. Jason was her spitting image.

"Yes," Jason said as he slowly nodded his head.

"Where to?" Kecia asked as she zipped out of the hospital's parking lot.

"School," Zola said. "We have to get Jason back to school before he gets in trouble."

"No," Jason whined. "I don't wanna go back there. I wanna stay with you."

Zola's heart raced. The last thing she wanted to do was send her son away. She always kept a strong façade, but living without Jason was something that weighed heavily on her mind every day, and now that he was here, combined with Carmen's shenanigans, she really wasn't in any rush to send him back.

"Okay. We'll do this," Zola said. "Why don't we go grab some lunch and then I'll take you back to school."

"But I don't wanna go back to school because Carmen will pick me up and after she finds out I ran away, she'll homeschool me. I never want to see her again. I hate her and she hates you," Jason said.

"Don't worry about Carmen. I can take care of myself," Zola said.

"I know a secret," Jason said, looking directly into his mother's face. "If I tell you, will you let me stay?"

"A secret?" Zola asked. "What kind of secret?"

"Can I stay with you?" Jason asked as if he was bargaining.

Zola frowned. There was something truly wrong with this picture. A child wasn't supposed to have to beg his mother to stay with her.

"Please," he said.

"Jason," she said as a tear welled up into the corner of her eye. "I need to do this the right way."

"This is the right way," he said.

"I can get in big trouble behind this," Zola said. "And I'm working to get you back with me permanently."

"Okay," Jason said, pouting. "But I'm only going to run away again. I hate Carmen. She's mean."

"No," Zola said. "I'm going to do what I have to do to get you back home with me but you have to promise me you'll help me. Do you promise?"

Jason looked out of the window and shook his head from side to side. He was a stubborn little boy.

Seeing her son with that look on his face, the look that said he didn't have any faith that she would save him from the evil Carmen, sent a wicked chill through her body. That was all she needed. It was time for a change of plans.

Ian pulled into his driveway around four-thirty in the morning. The moon was shining bright and sending a calming glow over the ghetto. A police car cruised up his street and slowed down before pointing his searchlight at Ian's truck. Ian opened the door, but before he could get out of his truck, a bright searchlight blasted his eyes.

"Everything okay, Ian?" a policeman working the graveyard shift asked as he turned the light off.

"Yeah. I'm good. Thanks for asking," Ian said to the officer.

"Up late tonight, Ian? Hot date?"

"No," Ian said. "I'm sitting here talking to my nephew."

"I hear ya. Have a good night, my friend," the officer said before pulling off down the street.

"It's quiet over here at night," KJ said.

"Only when the police are out," Ian said.

"They seem to know you well."

"Yeah. We try to look out for each other around here."

Ian stepped out of the truck and scanned the street. The presence of the police always sent the crackheads, prostitutes and other people of the night home early.

"Uncle Ian, I was over here the other day. I didn't know you lived here," KJ said as he stepped out of the truck and looked around the hood as if he was on a safari.

"What were you doing over here?" Ian asked.

"Just hanging out," he said.

"Just hanging out, huh? Who were you hanging out with?" Ian asked.

"Some friends from school," KJ said.

"Boy," Ian said, shaking his head. "You don't lie very well. But I'mma leave that one alone, for now."

KJ didn't try to defend himself, which bothered Ian. If he tried to fix his lie it would at least show he cared. But all KJ did was hunch his shoulders as if to say, take it or leave it.

They walked up the steps and onto the porch. Ian placed his key in the lock and opened the door. Once they were inside, he flipped on the lights, illuminating the small living room.

"I don't have a guest room, so you can take Christian's room or camp out on the sofa. Whatever you like."

KJ looked past Ian and out of the window at a human figure coming quickly toward his front door.

"Ian," the person said, knocking on the screen door.

Ian turned around just in time to see Trudy staring at him with wide eyes.

Trudy motioned with her hand for him to come outside as if she had a big secret and wasn't about to share it in front of a stranger.

Ian shook his head and stepped out onto the porch. "What do you want?"

"What you doing with that young boy in your house this time of night? You some kind of freak?"

"That's my nephew," he snapped. "What do you want, Trudy? Are you trying to get yourself shot? Running up on my porch this time of the morning."

"Nah," she said, looking around Ian's shoulder to get a good look at KJ. "You sure that's your nephew? I've never seen you with a woman, but damn. I don't associate with pedophiles."

"Man," Ian said, turning around to go back into his house.

"Wait," Trudy said. "A'ight, a'ight. I believe you. But listen. I'm trying to get some money."

"Well, keep trying. Good night," Ian said, turning to walk back into his house.

Trudy reached out and grabbed his arm.

"Get a job, Trudy."

"Job! Hell to the no. What I look like, getting a job? Then they might ask me to work," she said, shaking her head.

KJ came to the door. "Uncle Ian," he said, "where are the towels?"

"Ohh, your nephew's cute. How are you doing?"

K.J. frowned at the shell of a woman standing before him but waved his hand. "Hello," he said.

"Handsome li'l devil. You got a girlfriend?" Trudy asked.

"Yes, ma'am," K.J. said. "I'm good."

"I bet you are," Trudy said, flicking her tongue out at the minor. "Ian, you sure are having a whole lot of company lately. Where is Christian?"

"At my sister's house," he said. "What do you mean by that?"

"Sister? Boy, I didn't know you had a sister. Well, well, well, you learn something new every day. I guess that was your brother who came by here earlier."

"Brother? My brother was with me," Ian said with a frown.

"Oh well, some guy came by here looking for you," she said.

"What guy? What did he want?" Ian asked.

"I don't know. I didn't ask. He asked me if I seen you. But now that I think about it, he didn't say your name; just said something about your truck. He was a nice guy. Gave me a few dollars," Trudy said.

"What did he look like?" Ian asked.

"He was kind of sexy," Trudy said. "Look, man, I ain't got all night to be out here playing interviews. Now I need to hold a few dollars until I get my check."

"What check, Trudy? You been getting a check since I've known you and I haven't seen the first of any kind of payment back on one dime that I've given you."

"Oh, it's like that, Ian? Okay. I'mma remember that," Trudy said.

"Please do," Ian said. "Well, we're going to call it a night. You be careful out here."

"You ain't gonna give me a few bucks?"

"Trudy, I don't mind helping you out from time to time but I'm not going to be your human ready teller. You're going to have to get a job like everyone else."

"So you really ain't gonna give me a few dollars," Trudy said, confused because he had never turned her down before.

"Nope," he said. "I'm going to stop enabling you. You're one of the smartest people I know and I'm not going to keep helping you get high. Check yourself into rehab and get your life back."

"Aw, man," she said, sucking her raggedy teeth. "Here you go sounding like everybody else. I don't wanna hear that shit."

"You might not wanna hear that shit, but you need to," Ian said, opening his door. "Good night."

"That man that came by here looking for you," she said, pausing for effect, "he had a gun. I saw it with my own eyes. So you be careful."

Ian stared at the woman as she made her way down his driveway. A car drove by and the driver slowed down when he saw Trudy. He drove a few houses down from Ian and stopped. Trudy ran up and got into the passenger side. She was going to get her money the hard way. He wondered if she was telling the truth about the guy with the gun or if she was just upset that he didn't give her the money she requested. He closed the door and made sure the dead bolt was in place. He turned on the house alarm and walked back to his room.

"KJ," he said to the bathroom door. He heard the shower running. "Make yourself at home, nephew. I'm going to bed."

"Okay," KJ said over the running water.

"Why don't you take Christian's room and we'll talk in the morning."

"Okay," KJ said.

Ian grabbed his car keys and made sure his car was locked. Trudy had him on edge. He hit the automatic alarm on his Ford until he heard it chirp. Satisfied that his vehicle was safe, he walked back to his bedroom to retrieve his gun. Maybe Trudy was telling the truth. Either way, he wasn't taking any chances.

18

Ravon walked down the street and barely glanced at the house where all the murder and mayhem had taken place. His mother was dead and strangely enough everything seemed calm on the block. He looked around at the surrounding houses and realized that his mother's death was just business as usual in the hood. Death was nothing new to the ghetto residents; as a matter of fact, it was a way of life. Someone had placed a teddy bear on the front steps and that made him feel a little better. At least someone cared. He stopped walking and looked at the house that he came to visit. A light was on in a back room; he saw a television's blue screen dance off of the living room walls. A dog barked and ran full speed at him but stopped right before he ran into the chain link fence.

"Neko," he said, leaning over the fence to rub the dog's shaggy coat. "Have you forgotten about me?"

The dog wagged his tail and licked Ravon's hand.

Ravon looked to his left at his mother's house and couldn't help but think of how his mother looked when he saw her lying on the sofa. She seemed to have died in a lot of pain. Her mouth was twisted up into a menacing snarl; her hands were curled into little fists; and her eyes were still open. Then he remembered the blood. The floor was covered with it. He was amazed at how much blood could come from such a small woman.

Ravon took a deep breath and looked around to see if anyone

was watching before he opened the gate and walked up the concrete walkway leading up to the single family home. Neko followed him, begging to be rubbed, but Ravon kept walking up the cement stairs leading to Mrs. Ham's house. He knocked on the door and waited.

No answer, but he knew she was there. He knocked again. He could hear some movement inside.

"Who dat out dere?" the old woman from New Orleans asked in her heavy drawl.

"This is Ravon. Ravon from next door. Sara's son," he said.

"Hey, baaaabe," she said. "Whatcha want dis time of night?"

"I have a quick question," he said. "I promise you I won't hold you long."

The door clicked as locks were disengaged. A few seconds later, the door opened. Mrs. Ham stood behind the screen door wearing a nightgown, a housecoat that hung on her skinny frame like a hanger, and an array of colorful rollers in her gray hair.

"Whatcha need, chile?" she said through the bars on the window on the storm door.

"I'm sorry to come by here so late, but I'm trying to find out what happened next door," Ravon said.

"I don't know nothing but what I told the police," she said.

"What was that?" Ravon said, hoping she hadn't mentioned his name.

"The last person I seen coming from over there was your sister. That was when I saw you that day, but I didn't see you go inside. You talked to me; then you left. That's all I know," Mrs. Ham said. "Now I don't want any trouble. I like to mind my own business, so I would appreciate it if you don't put me in this mess."

"That's all you know?"

"Yep," she said, backing away from the door. "Now I need to get back to bed."

"Okay," Ravon said. "Thank you for answering the door this time of night and I'm sorry for waking you."

Mrs. Ham nodded her head but stood staring at Ravon. He could tell there was something else the old woman wanted to tell him.

Ravon didn't move.

"Listen," she said. "There was this car that dropped your sister off. One of those truck things that I see on my cop shows. I got the license plate. I didn't give this to the police 'cause like I said, I like to mind my business. But you wait right there. Now I don't know if this will help you, but you wait right there."

Ravon waited on the porch. Mrs. Ham closed her door and Ravon heard the locks click back into place.

He turned around and looked over at his mother's house. The only thing that let on that a crime had taken place there was a few strips of yellow police tape around the front door and carport. He thought back to the man who he had found in the house and couldn't help but wonder what kind of foolishness his mother was caught up in. He scratched his head and wished he had known more about the woman who gave birth to him. He remembered when he was in prison and she wrote him a letter. It was the only letter he'd ever received from her in the five years that he was there, but it spoke volumes on what made her tick.

Dear Ravon,

I hope this letter finds you in good health and spirits. I know you didn't expect to hear from me and to be honest with you, I don't know why I'm writing you. I guess when you give birth to somebody, you should act like you care. Truth is, I do care, but to be honest with you, I never wanted kids. I don't like kids and I especially don't like girl children. I really don't like people. People are evil and over the years I think I can honestly say that I found that out myself. I believe the world we live in is hell and heaven is waiting in the afterlife. I grew up in

California and when I was a teenager I joined the Black Panther Party for Social and Economic Change. I met a man and I guess I fell in love. We moved to Atlanta to start a branch here, but something changed once we got here. He fell out of love with the struggle and in love with heroine. I still tried to be there for him, but he was cursed. On the day Zola was born, he left and the only time I saw him after that was in my nightmares. You have a different daddy and I don't have any idea who he is. I was a zombie walking around and meeting men just to keep me company, but most of them were evil and selfish and mere products of this world we live in. I never met my own parents; they decided I wasn't worth sticking around for. I grew up in a California orphanage where I met hundreds, maybe even thousands, of black faces who was just like me. I was treated okay. No physical or sexual abuse for me, but when I turned seventeen, they cut me loose, and to me that was its own kind of abuse. They sent a skinny little girl out into this cruel world to fend for herself and I was promptly physically abused by the state of California. That's when I joined the movement. I needed a family to protect me and the Panthers offered that. But even that wasn't all it was cracked up to be. We started out strong, but drugs were flooded into our neighborhoods and we weren't smart enough to avoid it. Over the years, seeing how my people have virtually destroyed their lives, I took on the notion to help them finish the job. Everywhere I turn, I see black faces not caring about prosperity or their families. There is no self-love. The folks that have money look down on the ones who don't and the ones that don't have it hate the ones that have it. That's why they rob and kill and rape and so on and so on. I bet if you take a look around that prison you are in, you will see mostly black faces. Why do you think that's the case? Black people are cursed. You've always been a good boy, yet you are sitting there with some of the world's worst people. Why do you think that's the case? You've always gotten good grades. You even got a few academic scholarship offers, but where are you? And why? If you were any other race, the judge would've slapped you on the wrist and said, don't do that anymore; but you are Black, and probation was too good for you. I can't tell you the number of times I wanted to kill us all, because this world isn't meant for us. But for whatever reason, I believe in my own higher power and that is one of the sins that I think is unforgivable. Well, I wanted to write you and let you know who I really am. I'm not a bad person; I'm a cursed one.

Sara.

PS. If you talk to your sister, tell her I don't hate her but that I'm not fit to be anyone's mother. Medication altered my way of thinking when I did what I did to her and I will never forgive myself for that, but she has to move on and live her life. She came by here a few days ago but I couldn't bring myself to open the door. She's a big-hearted girl and I really hate myself even more when I see her. I'm full of evil spirits, son. And that was an evil spirit that tried to ruin her from having any kids. Crazy as it sounds, I was trying to look out for her. So pray for me, pray for us all. God has a special place for us.

"Baaabe," Mrs. Ham said, bringing Ravon back to the here and now. "Here is the paper I wrote the license plate number on. I didn't give this to the police because something told me not to. You can't trust them and the ones they sent 'round here seemed a little crooked."

"Hard to find a good one," Ravon said.

"Yeah, I always listen to my first thought, but maybe you can do something with it and find out if that man knows something. I didn't get along with Sara too well but she didn't deserve that."

Ravon thought about how the two women would stare at each other and never utter a word, one not liking the other for no apparent reason.

"Thanks, Mrs. Ham," Ravon said, staring down at the paper and trying to make out the chicken scratch she called writing. "Is this a G or an O?"

Mrs. Ham laughed, squinted her wrinkled eyelids, then shook her head. "I don't know."

"Okay," he said. "I'll figure it out. You take care of yourself now."

"I sho' will," she said. "I'm glad you taking care of your momma. She was a mean old bitch, but she was still yo' momma."

"Yeah." Ravon nodded and turned to walk down the steps of the front porch. "You be careful around here."

"I will," she said. "And you do the same. Hey, Ravon."

"Yes, ma'am," he said, stopping and turning around to face her.

"I saw you leaving the house the other day. It was right after I heard those gun shots," she said, pointing her boney finger at him.

Ravon stared at the woman without saying a word. His heart hit the floor. The first thing he thought about was going back to prison. That wasn't going to happen. Her next words would decide if she lived or died. He had killed once and didn't feel the slightest bit of remorse and he was sure this kill wouldn't cause him much discomfort either.

"But they say yo' momma was stabbed to death. And the white man was shot. If there is one thing I know about yo' momma, it's that she didn't have much love in her heart for white peoples. So I know that cracker wasn't making a social call. So I had to ask myself, what was his pale ass doing up in there? I say that to say, your secret is safe with me. I don't blame you for what you done and you ain't got to worry about me telling a soul."

Ravon grunted and nodded his head. He wasn't sure if she was wearing a wire and working for the police. He wasn't saying anything to incriminate himself. "You take care of yourself, Mrs. Ham."

"Oh, don't you worry about me. You take care of yourself. And I hope your momma is finally at peace," she said, closing her door and sliding all of the locks back into place.

19

Zola opened the door to her condominium and stepped back to allow Jason and Kecia to enter before her.

"I'm going to grab a few things; then I can get my butt to work," Kecia said as she made a beeline to the guestroom.

"I thought you were off today," Zola said as she looked around her place to see if anything was out of place.

"I am, but I'm a student, girl. Do you know how much work I have to do? I'm never off. When I'm supposed to be off, I'm studying. Heck, who am I kidding? Even when I'm at work, I'm working and I'm studying. Besides, I never liked being a third wheel. You guys need to spend some time together. I have plenty to keep me busy," she said as she disappeared.

Jason walked around and checked out his mom's place. He walked over by the large wall-length window and looked down at the cars racing up and down Moreland Avenue. "I wanna stay here," he said to no one in particular. "I don't want to go back over there with them."

Zola heard the pain in her son's voice and felt helpless to do anything to ease it. She knew she couldn't just pick up the phone and call the Benjamins and tell them, "I'll take it from here."

Kecia rushed out of the guest room. She said her goodbyes to the both of them and was hustling toward the door. Zola waved, but her attention was on Jason. Their eyes met and Zola saw his eyes begging her to save him from whatever had him so ill at ease. But what had happened? The last few times she had visited him, he seemed to be enjoying himself so much that she walked away feeling like she wasn't a true part of his life.

Zola walked over to the window and stood beside her son. "I really want you to stay with me, too, Jason," she said. "But things are a little complicated. Will you tell me why you don't want to stay with the Benjamins anymore?"

"They're not nice. Well, Mr. Chad is okay, but Carmen is mean. She always talks about you. She told me that I wasn't going to see you ever again and that I needed to get used to it. She drinks a lot, too. She's weird. I don't like her."

"Has she ever hit you?" Zola asked.

"No," Jason said, shaking his head. "She keeps saying she loves me and she doesn't want you to have me. And I feel weird having white parents when I go to school. I feel like a pet."

"Well, you have been with them for a long time and she probably does love you," Zola said.

"I know, but I'm your son. I'm not their son. Do you have a room for me?"

There was something about the way he said that that made her want to cry.

"Of course," she said. "You *are* my son. It doesn't matter where you're spending your days and nights, I'll always have a room for you. Why do you think I got a two-bedroom place? One for me and one for you," she said with a smile.

Jason smiled. He reached out and hugged his mother's waist. Something caught his eye and he pulled away and walked over to the coffee table. He picked up a picture frame and stared at it. Inside the frame was a picture of Zola and Andre.

"Why do you have a picture of Mr. Andy?" he asked.

Zola frowned. *Mr. Andy?*

"Who?" she asked. "His name is Andre and he's my friend."

"No," Jason said, shaking his head. "That's Mr. Andy and he

works for the Benjamins. He used to be the driver. He used to take me to school every day, but now he does something else and I hardly ever see him anymore."

"Jason, are you sure that this is the same guy?" Zola asked, taking the picture from him and pointing at Andre.

"Yes," he said. "He has a cut over his lip. He told me he got that playing football."

He told me he got it in a car accident, she thought.

"He was at the house before I left. Somebody beat him up and I overheard him arguing with Carmen. He was telling her he wasn't going to do something and she got mad. I mean really mad. Then he left."

Zola's heart hit the carpet as she wondered what Andre could possibly have to do with Carmen. Her mind was racing and she felt betrayed.

Zola walked over and turned on the television. "What's your favorite show?" she asked while handing him the remote control.

"*Everybody Hates Chris*, but it's not on," Jason said, taking a seat on the plush leather sofa.

"Well, have at it. I need to make a phone call," she said as she went into her bedroom.

Zola grabbed her cell phone and called Sharon Capers, the attorney, and explained her situation. She told her about what Jason said about "Andre" and the coincidence of him beating her, then ending up at the Benjamins arguing with Carmen. Sharon told her that she would look into it, but in the meantime she needed to get Jason back over to the Benjamins' house.

"I can't do that," Zola said. "I think he may be in danger."

"Well, then we need to get the police involved. And you said you never relinquished full custody?" Sharon responded. "Only temporary, right?"

"Right," Zola said. "I would never give up the rights to my child.

That would never happen in a million years. I don't care how poor I was or how rich the Benjamins are, he's my son."

"Okay. I understand," Sharon said. "In the meantime, you call the police and tell them you believe Jason is in danger. You tell them everything that you know. Don't hold back anything to try and protect this 'Andre' guy because it's pretty obvious that he's not who he said he is and he's working for her. You're still his mother and you have rights. I will have a private investigator look into the Benjamins and if you hear or can think of anything that might help build a case against them, let me know. It doesn't matter how small or insignificant you may think it is, let me know."

"Okay," Zola said.

"Hang in there, Zola. I know you've been through a lot, but you're a fighter and if there is anything worth fighting for, it's your son," Sharon said.

"You're right about that," she said. "And thanks again, Sharon. You're the best."

"Don't mention it," Sharon said.

Zola ended the call with the attorney and sat on the edge of her bed. Everything she had with Andre was a lie. He was a liar. She felt like a fool for some of the things she did for him, all in the name of love. All kinds of emotions raced through her body. Fear, anger, resentment, embarrassment, hate, but the one that kept overriding the others was betrayal. She had been used once again. Tears formed in the corners of her eyes and raced down her cheeks.

Her mind drifted back to the crazy lady who was screaming at her the day she left Sara's house.

Was she really cursed?

All of a sudden, Zola was happy that she had insisted that the deed to the condo and the title to the car both be placed in her name when "Andre" bought them. She now had a car and a condo that were paid for and all because the Benjamins wanted her out of the picture. She was going to make sure she stayed one step ahead of them. She looked at her BlackBerry, then sighed. It was time. She dialed 9-1-1. It was time to get this situation resolved once and for all.

"Nine-one-one, what's your emergency?"

"My son is in danger," Zola said in a calm and cool fashion. There was a peace that ran through her veins like never before. "There are some wealthy and powerful people who want to take him from me. I need to speak with a police officer right now."

20

Ravon sat with his eyes trained on the house across the street. It was almost four in the morning and he had been sitting there for three-and-a-half hours. After he left Mrs. Ham's house, he got a stroke of luck when Lisa called. He had her pull the license plate number that the old woman had gotten. He wasn't sure how she did it but she called him back with an address and the owner's name. It didn't take long for him to find the place because he knew the West End area of Atlanta from when he was a kid. He backed into the driveway of an abandoned house across the street.

His mind was racing a million miles a minute when, all of a sudden, a Ford Explorer pulled into the driveway. Ravon's hands began to sweat as he sat there watching. There was someone in the passenger side, but they didn't get out of the car. A police officer drove by and he slid down in the seat. When he looked up again, the driver and someone else were out of the car and on the porch.

There was that woman again, the same woman who had walked up to him begging for money. He had given her five dollars and asked her a few softball questions about the man who owned the house. She claimed she didn't know him but there she was talking to him. He was willing to bet that she was warning him. He gripped his pistol and prepared himself for the unknown. This man may have the answers to the questions that were running rampant through his mind or he may have been the Good Samaritan that Zola claimed he was. The other guy walked into the house, but the man was still on the porch talking to the woman.

He wondered what they had to talk about at this hour. Then the woman ran off and jumped into a car. The man on the porch paused and looked up and down the street before going into his house. Ravon slumped back down in the driver's seat to avoid the man's gaze. He wasn't sure if he saw him or not. What now? He needed to talk to that guy, but he didn't think it was a good time. He eased his seat back and decided he would wait until daybreak. His eyes were getting heavy. He hadn't been to sleep in almost twenty-four hours. He locked his doors, cracked his windows, made sure his pistol was loaded and ready to go, and then fell asleep.

21

I an turned the television off and picked up a book called *Say
You Are One of Them*, a book of short stories about some folks
in Africa and some of the things they go through on a daily
basis. The story he was reading was called "Fattening the Gabon,"
a very interesting story of an uncle who had a change of heart
about selling his niece and nephew to a group of child traffickers.
He enjoyed reading, novels in particular. The written word had
a way of helping him to forget about the many problems that
were always present between his ears. So, every night before he
went to sleep, he made sure to read a few chapters written by
some of this world's best griots. After about thirty minutes of
reading, he was tired. He couldn't read another sentence, so he
reached over, placed his book on the nightstand and turned off
the lamp. As he lay there, he couldn't help but think about the
night he had had with his family. In one night, he experienced all
of the things he had really missed about his family: laughter,
good food, great conversations, drama, and family love. He smiled
when he thought about how happy Christian was as he ran around
his sister's house. He reached over, picked up his cell phone and
dialed her number.

"Hello," Andrea said with a sleep-filled voice.

"Did I wake you?"

"Yes," she said. "Is everything okay? Is KJ alright?"

He was happy to hear the concern in her voice about her son.

"Yeah," he said. "He's fine. Did Christian wake up?"

"No," she said. "But I'll tell you what. If he kicks me one more time, I'm going to pick up his li'l butt and put him in KJ's stinky room."

Ian laughed. "Yeah, he sleeps wild."

"What you doing calling here this time of morning?"

"I was just checking on you guys."

"Stop lying, boy. You were checking to see if Christian woke up wanting you. He's not thinking about you."

"Yes, he is. He's dreaming about me right now," Ian said.

"I'm sure he is. Now if you don't mind, I'd like to get back to dreaming about Denzel Washington."

"Okay," Ian said with a grunt. "Tomorrow. Well, later today, we need to talk about the way you've been treating KJ."

"The way I've been treating KJ?" Andrea almost yelled. "Ian, you've been missing in action for a long time. Don't let that boy fool you. He's not as innocent as he makes himself out to be."

"I don't care about any of that. What I do care about is the way you are carrying on. You should be ashamed of yourself, Andrea."

"You got a lot of nerve, popping your tail up, pointing fingers at me. I've been through hell and high water trying to make sure that boy has a good life and all he does is give me his butt to kiss."

"Andrea," Ian said, "I'm not about to get into any of that. You are projecting and I don't like it. Every time you see KJ, you see his dad. And you can't seem to get over what his dad did, but that was his dad; not KJ. I know you're angry, but you have to stop beating up on him because of the sins of his father."

"Oh, you are so wrong. I beat up on KJ because he acts like an ass ninety percent of the time."

"Have you ever wondered why? Have you ever tried to see

things from his perspective? He got shafted in this deal, too. It's not all about you. As matter of fact, this doesn't have a damn thing to do with you. His dad didn't just leave you for another man; he left him, too. And for a son, that has to be hard."

Andrea sighed on the other end of the phone as if she wasn't trying to hear Ian's logic.

"Cut the boy some slack," Ian said. "It's bad enough he has to live with the fact that his father left him, but he left to be with another man. And on top of that, his mother is treating him like shit. Now, if you need some time to yourself, he can stay with me."

There was silence on the other end, so he went on.

"You don't have to make a decision right now, but just know that I'm here. And I'm not going to allow you to mistreat him anymore."

"I hear ya, Ian. I'm sleepy. Good night," Andrea said before hanging up.

Ian held the phone in his hand and wished he hadn't been such a stranger. His nephew was over there getting mentally abused by his scorned mother and he was somewhere wrapped up in his own selfish bubble. He placed his phone on the nightstand and stared up at the ceiling illuminated by the fading moon.

Ian's mind shifted to the guy who was asking questions about him. He wondered if he was still parked across the street. Who was he? Why was he asking Trudy about him? Was Trudy lying just to get a few bucks out of him? No, that wasn't like her. Was he a trick getting his rocks off with one of the many crackheads who strolled up and down Ralph David Abernathy Boulevard, or was he a threat? He slid his hand under his mattress and removed his 9 millimeter pistol.

Ian looked up and saw it was almost six o'clock in the morning. He was tired, but this guy had his mind racing, so he stood up and walked to the front of his house to see if the watcher was still there. He peered through the wooden shades over the bay window and saw that the guy's car was still there. He wasn't being very inconspicuous. Ian decided he would sit back and let this guy come to him. He walked back to his room and got back in bed. It didn't take long for him to drift off into a sound and peaceful sleep.

22

Ravon opened his eyes and was surprised to see that the night had already given way to morning. His windows were foggy and he was freezing. He got out of his car to stretch his legs and get a breath of fresh air. He turned and stared at the house across the street. The SUV was still in the driveway and all of the lights inside of the house were off. His bladder was begging to be relieved so he walked toward the back of the empty house where he had parked and unzipped his pants. Just as he was finishing up, he heard something behind him and he quickly turned around.

"Good morning," a voice said, startling him.

Ravon whipped his head around and stared at the raggedy looking man who was standing on the steps of the deck. He fiddled around for his gun but realized he'd left it in the car.

"Whatchu doing round here, boy? What's your name?" said Ian's neighbor, Willie.

Ravon's eyes left the man's haggard-looking face and found the long silver samurai sword he was holding as if he was going to swing it at his neck if he didn't get the answer to his question. Ravon zipped his pants and ran back to his car. When he opened the door, he searched for the gun he had left on the passenger seat but it was gone.

"You looking for this?" Harry, Ian's other neighbor, asked, holding Ravon's pistol.

"Man," Ravon said, outnumbered and outgunned. "What y'all want with me?"

"I wanna know why you've been hanging in my driveway all night long."

"I was sleeping and I didn't know this was your house. I thought it was empty," Ravon said.

"I hope nobody pays you for thinking," Willie said.

"I wanna know why you asking questions about my friend," Harry said.

"Who?" Ravon asked with a frown.

"Who?" Willie snapped and pointed the sword at Ravon. "Who in the hell you've been asking about?"

"I...I...I," Ravon stammered. Even though the old men seemed like harmless bums, he wasn't taking any chances because that sword was real and it looked sharp.

"I...I...I... Hell. Get ya lies straight, fool," Willie said.

"Ain't nobody gonna hurt you," Harry said, waving Ravon's gun in his face.

"Speak for yourself. I ain't take my damn meds and I'm a li'l fucked up in the head right now, so I wouldn't put it past me to take this damn sword and chop ya li'l narrow ass up. And I'll get away with it, too, because all these police 'round here know I'm a li'l off," Willie said as he lifted the sword up over his head. "Now, I'mma ask you one more time. Whatcha doing round here?"

"Whoa, man. I'm not looking for any trouble. Somebody killed my mother and I wanted to know who that guy was because he dropped my sister off at her house. My sister and my mother don't speak, so it's odd and all I wanted to do was ask him some questions to see if he could help lead me in the right direction," Ravon said.

"Well, we don't have no killers on this block," Willie snapped.

"Yeah, we do," Harry corrected. "Mrs. Hazel's son, Bobby, killed those folks that time he tried to rob the check-cashing joint over there on Martin Luther King."

"And his ass is underneath the jail," Willie said. "And why you snitching, man?"

"He ain't locked up no more," Harry said, shaking his head. "I saw him last week at the Laundromat."

"What the hell you doing at the Laundromat?" Willie asked.

Ravon swiveled his head back and forth as the men carried on their own conversation.

"What the hell you think I was doing at the Laundromat? What people do at the Laundromat, Willie?"

"I know what people do, but what the hell you doing there? You wear the same dirty ass shirt every day."

"Ya momma wear the same drawls," Harry snapped.

"Hey," Willie said, turning his sword on Harry. "My momma dead."

"Well, hell. I know for sure she wearing the same drawls then," Harry said as he turned to Ravon. "You ever see a dead mother-fucker change drawls?"

"Hey," Ravon said, raising his hands to stay out of this conversation.

"What the hell you got to say about my momma?" Willie said, turning toward Ravon.

"Nothing. Can I leave?"

"Hell no. We ain't done with you. Now if you wanted to talk to the man, why didn't you just walk yo' li'l ass over there and knock on the door?"

"Yeah," Harry added. "Why you out here looking all like you tryna rob somebody? We don't play that. We keep this street safe."

"I'm not trying to rob anybody," Ravon said.

"Of course you gonna say that. I ain't ever met a nukka who admitted to ·trynna rob somebody. You think we some kind of fools?"

"No," Ravon said. "It's not like that. I'm telling y'all the truth."

Willie looked at Harry while still holding the sword above his head. "You believe this fool?"

Harry leaned in close to Ravon's face and Ravon backed up due to the stench coming from the bum's raggedy mouth.

"Yeah," Harry said. "I think he's telling the truth. I'm keeping this gun, but I think he's telling the truth. We don't need to kill him."

Willie lowered his weapon and smiled at Ravon.

"I'll tell you what," Willie said. "You do realize we got the drop on ya, don't you?"

"I guess so," Ravon said.

"You got some money?" Willie asked.

"I have a few bucks," Ravon said.

"How much is a few bucks?" Harry added.

"About fifty dollars," Ravon said, figuring that number would satisfy them.

"Okay," Willie said. "Get in the car. We going to IHOP and you buying, damn it. I got a taste for some of those sweet-ass pancakes."

"Huh?" Ravon said.

"You heard me, damn it," Willie said, lifting his sword again. "We kidnapping yo' ass and making you take us to breakfast."

"Yeah," Harry said. "I want some French toast and bacon. And maybe we can answer some of your questions."

"I ain't answering shit," Willie said. "I already let this fool live."

"Don't pay him no mind," Harry said. "He wasn't lying about them meds. Trust me on that one."

"Man," Ravon said with a frown. "Why don't I just give y'all the money and y'all go on your own."

"Nope," Willie said. "You're taking us, because if you look around, you won't see a car. My BMW is being detailed."

"I don't have time to take y'all to no IHOP," Ravon said.

"You got time to die?" Willie snapped. "Well, a'ight then. Get your skinny tail in this car and turn on the heat. I'm colder than an ice cube in a polar bear's ass."

Ravon shook his head and wondered what in the world had he gotten himself into.

23

The morning sun was creeping through Zola's window as she rolled over and looked at the smooth face of her sleeping son. During the night, he had slept peacefully, even cuddling up close to her like he did when he was a toddler. So much was on her mind and she tossed and turned all night. She felt as if she was stealing her own child because every little sound she heard sent her heart racing. She had called the police to report her concerns about Jason's welfare just as her attorney had instructed her to do, but that didn't make her feel any better. Now another day was upon them and she could only imagine what it would bring.

Zola reached over to the nightstand and unplugged her cell phone from the charger. She looked at the screen of her BlackBerry and noticed that she had eleven missed calls and all of them were from Carmen Benjamin. She checked her voicemail and heard Carmen's panic-filled voice.

"Zola," the woman said, "Jason has disappeared. We have an Amber Alert out. We are doing everything we can to locate him. He walked away from school today and no one has seen him. Oh my God. I'm so scared," she said.

The next message was a little different. "Zola," Carmen's voice echoed with a different tone. "I hope Jason is not with you. If you took my son, that's right, I said, *my* son, you will regret the day you were ever born."

Six or seven more messages followed with similar words. Zola looked back at her son and leaned down and kissed his forehead. She stood and walked down the hallway. She stuck her head into the guestroom to see if Kecia had made it in, but the room was empty and the bed was untouched.

She walked into the kitchen and poured herself a glass of orange juice. Just as she was about to take a swallow, her cell phone rang.

"Hello," she said.

"Zola. Are you okay?"

"Ravon," she asked. "Where have you been?"

"Man," he said with an exasperated breath. "Don't even ask. How are you?"

"I'm fine. I called you a million times. I needed a ride to the hospital."

"Damn," he said. "I'm sorry, Zo. I was with Lisa and I promised her when I was locked up that I would spend a few days with her with no distractions. Then I lost my cell phone. Are you okay?"

"I'm getting there. Did you hear about Sara?"

"Yeah," he said. "What's going on? I need to talk to you in person. I don't trust these phones."

"I understand. Those sorry police officers showed up to the hospital room and tried to pin it on me. I have an attorney now, so hopefully she can straighten this mess out. Sara gives me hell even in her death."

"Hey," Ravon said. "Can you meet me somewhere?"

"I have Jason here and I'm still not really comfortable driving. Why? What's going on?"

"I don't know," he said, sounding a bit panicky. "Maybe I shouldn't be out and about. Next thing I know they'll be trying to pin it on me. I'm not going back to prison. Fuck that."

"Are you okay, Ray? You sound strange."

"Yeah. I'm straight. Listen. I will be in touch with you. I gotta figure some things out."

"Ray," Zola said, but the phone went dead.

There was a knock on the door.

"Ray," Zola said as she stood and made her way over to the door.

Zola looked through the tiny peephole in her door and frowned at what was on the other side.

She opened the door and looked into the eyes of Detective Shilo. She looked to his left, then his right for his pessimistic partner, but the detective was alone.

"May I come in?" he asked.

"I didn't kill anybody," she snapped. "And I would appreciate it if ya'll leave me alone."

"I know," he said, holding up his hands to fend off the verbal onslaught that was coming his way.

"If you know that, then why are you here harassing me?"

"I'm not here to harass you. I only want to ask you a few questions," he said. "I'm here on my own accord. I'm not here to accuse you of anything. I didn't approve of my partner's methods one bit, but he's been on the force way longer than I have so I had to play my position. But I would like to have a few words with you, if you don't mind."

Zola stared into the man's eyes and he seemed sincere. She backed away from the door and allowed him to enter. She kept her mean face on and made sure he knew that he was on a short clock.

"Make it quick. I have things to do," she said as she walked over and folded up the blanket that was spread out on the sofa. She took the blanket back to her bedroom and peeked in on her son.

"I'll try not to take up too much of your time, Ms. Zaire," Detective Shilo said as he walked over to the end table and picked up the same picture of Andre that Jason had. "How well do you know this man?"

"I guess not as well as I thought I did," she said. "Why?"

"Is this the same man?" Detective Shilo asked as he produced his own picture.

Zola studied the picture of the man who claimed he loved her. Both of his eyes were swollen, his top lip was almost doubled in size and there was a nasty cut across his nose.

"Yeah," she said, nodding her head. "That looks like him."

"Thank you," Shilo said as he slid the picture back in his suit breast pocket. He nodded his head and looked at her as if she was going to share a little more information.

"Is that it?"

"He paid us a visit last night. Someone or something got a hold of him and he's scared out of his mind."

That got her attention.

"He shared some things, but I know he's holding back."

"Did he kill Sara?"

"I don't think so," Detective Shilo, said shaking his head. "But then again, I don't know. He kept mumbling something about how he didn't sign up for people getting killed. He said *people*. Last I checked, your mother was only one person. We only found one body at the crime scene but there was another person who died in that house. We have gunshot casings and lots of blood in the kitchen. Too much blood for the person to have survived so somebody moved the other body."

Zola stared at the man, hanging onto his every word. She couldn't bring herself to mourn her mother, but she was still interested in how she had met her demise.

"Your friend here," Detective Shilo said, tapping the frame. "I think he knows more than he's telling and some of the things he's saying are lies, which is why I'm here. How long have you known Mr. Dubois?"

"Not long enough to know that was his last name. What is his first?"

"Andy. Andy Dubois. He's from Cleveland, Ohio. He did a few years in prison for various petty crimes. He likes to find wealthy women and prey on them."

"Well, I'm far from wealthy, so he had the wrong one."

"I know," he said, and swept his eyes around the opulent pad and nodded his head. "You were not his target, but from the looks of this place you have here, you seem to be doing okay for yourself."

"Who was his target?"

"That's why I'm here. I need a little help. The people who keep your son, what kind of relationship do you have with them?"

I thought I had a pretty good one until that bitch tried to poison my son against me, she thought, but since he was a police officer and she didn't trust anyone who worked for the judicial system, she just hunched her shoulders.

"My son told me he works for the people who are caring for him. He said he heard him arguing with Carmen."

"And Carmen is his stepmother," Detective Shilo said as he pulled out his mini writing pad.

"She's just a caregiver. I'm my son's mother."

"I see," Detective Shilo said, nodding his head. "Well, Mr. Dubois claims he wanted to stop working for them, but when I asked him what he did for them, he started stuttering."

"Why did he come to you?"

"He seems to think someone is trying to kill him. He said his car blew up and he was kidnapped, beaten, and left for dead. I haven't been able to confirm the car story, but his broken arm, leg and facial lacerations tell me there may be a little truth to his story."

"I see," Zola said, shaking her head at what she was hearing. "So what does all of this have to do with me? Do you think I tried to kill him, too?"

"Nope," Detective Shilo said. "I thought I was clear when I said I wasn't here to accuse you of anything."

"So all you wanted to know was how I knew Andre? Or Andy... whatever you said his name was?"

"Yes, and anything else you could tell me."

"I can tell you that I don't think my child is safe with Carmen Benjamin and I'm not sending him back over there."

Detective Shilo nodded his head as if to say he worked homicide, not domestic cases. "I'm sorry to hear that. Have you called down to the station to report your concerns?"

"Yes."

"Well, they should take care of it."

"Yeah. I won't hold my breath waiting on Atlanta P.D. to come to my rescue."

"Thank you for your time, Ms. Zaire, and I hope you get better soon."

Zola nodded and walked him to the door.

As she opened the door to let Detective Shilo out, she found two hulking uniformed police officers staring at her with stern faces. The white officer wore shades and had a crew cut. The black guy was dark as the night and seemed to be ready to shoot her.

"Zola Zaire, we're here to pick up Jason Zaire," the black officer said. "You are in violation of a court order and if you don't produce the child, you will be arrested for kidnapping."

Zola looked at Detective Shilo for help, but he was already walking down the hallway toward the elevator.

"You're not taking my son," Zola said.

"Ma'am, please step aside," Crew Cut said.

"I can't do that," she said. "I just called the police and explained to them that my child is in danger."

"Ma'am, we're not going to ask you again," the black guy said as he removed his taser.

Zola looked into the man's eyes and couldn't find a trace of compassion. She pushed the door closed and Crew Cut caught it with his black steel-toed boot. The black officer stuck his hand through the door and let off 50,000 volts of electricity directly into her already frail body.

The shock was like something she had never felt before. Her entire body locked up and seemed to go into cardiac arrest. She lay on the floor helplessly as the two officers rushed into her bedroom. When she looked up, Crew Cut was carrying her son in his arms. Jason looked around, then noticed his mother on the floor and started screaming.

"Mom!" the little boy screamed. "Mommmmmmmm!"

The sound was heart wrenching but she couldn't move to do anything to stop them. The black officer stood over her, staring down at her like he had just stepped on a roach. Zola looked up at him and pleaded with her eyes for him to leave her child alone, but all she got was a blank stare in return. She tried to speak, but her brain didn't seem to get the message. The next thing she heard was the door closing and her son was gone.

24

Ian worked his way around the kitchen. He was cooking a late brunch of grits, eggs, turkey sausage, and raisin toast. After he poured two glasses of orange juice, he walked down the hallway and knocked on Christian's door.

"Good morning, KJ," Ian said, opening the bedroom's door.

KJ rolled over and looked around as if he was in a bad dream. He jerked his head from left to right, then he settled on his uncle. He squinted as he zeroed in on the familiar looking face.

"Hey, Uncle Ian," he said, finally finding his bearing and relaxing a little.

"It's time to rise and shine, my man. A fresh washcloth is in the bathroom on the shelf. I've already cooked, so hop to it before your food gets cold."

KJ rolled over and sat on the side of the bed. He looked around the room and saw a slew of toy cars on a desk. He smiled and remembered back when he was a toy fanatic. His dad would buy him anything and everything he could dream of. He stood and sighed at how drastically things had changed between him and the man who had meant everything to him. KJ walked to the bathroom and relieved himself, then washed his hands and face. He used the brand-new toothbrush that was sitting on the marble countertop to clean his teeth and freshen his breath before walking out into the kitchen.

"Good morning," Ian said. "I hope you're hungry."

"Yeah," KJ said. "I'm starving."

"Good," Ian said as he placed a loaded plate in front of his nephew and took a seat across from him.

"How long can I stay with you?" KJ asked.

"How long would you like to stay?"

"Forever," he said. "My mother hates me and my dad doesn't even care enough to hate me; I'm not a fan of either one of them, so it's best if I just stay away."

"That's not true. Both of your parents love you."

"You can love someone and not like them. Like, I love my mom, but I don't like her. I don't like my dad and I'm not sure I even love him."

"You and your dad were always very close so I think you are just angry or disappointed with him. Like you said, you can love and not like."

"Yeah, maybe," KJ said as he dropped his head and said his grace.

"So is that why you are dabbling in drugs?"

KJ's eyes grew wide as silver dollars.

"Yeah," Ian said, "you didn't think you were hiding it, did you?"

KJ didn't answer.

"Well, I'm not going to sit here and preach, but make that your last time doing that. Just because you're not happy with the way things are going in your life doesn't mean you quit living. And when you dabble in drugs, you are telling the world that you have checked out of life."

There was a loud commotion out on the front porch. Ian wiped his mouth with a cloth napkin and stood up. He walked out through the living room and opened the door.

"What's going on out here, fellas?"

Willie and Harry were flanking some guy who looked like he wanted to strangle both of them.

"What's going on? I'll tell ya what's going on. This man here says you murdered his mother," Willie said.

"No, he didn't," Harry said. "He said he wanted to talk to Ian because Ian knows who murdered his mother. Damn, Willie. Why don't you get your facts straight?"

"I didn't say either one of those things. And get y'all hands off of me. I already took y'all to IHOP and the liquor store. Now will y'all let me talk to this man in peace?"

Willie looked at Harry as if to see if it was okay to release their prisoner.

"Give me five dollars and I'll let you go," Harry said.

"I ain't giving y'all another dime and get your dirty hands off of me."

"Hey, hey, hey," Ian said. "I'll take it from here, guys."

Willie held up his hands and Harry held out his. "Five dollars, nukka?"

"Bye, Harry," Ian said. "I'll make sure I give you a li'l something a little later."

The two drunks left the porch and nodded their heads because they knew Ian's word was as good as gold. Ian walked out on his front porch to join his visitor. He looked out into the street and noticed the same car parked out by his mailbox as the one he had seen earlier.

"What's up?"

"My name is Ravon Zaire and I understand you dropped my sister off at my mom's house. My mom ended up dead and I was wondering if you knew anything that might help me find out what's going on?"

"I'm not sure that I can help you, my friend. I just dropped her off. I don't know your sister or your mother. I met her that day that I gave her the ride. Is she okay?"

"Yeah," Ravon said. "She's fine."

"Why don't you go to the police for your answers?"

"I can't. Well, I shouldn't say that I can't; it's just that I don't feel comfortable."

"Why not?" Ian asked.

"I'll be honest with you. I just got out of prison and I don't trust the police. She said you were nice to her."

Ian stared at the guy, not sure what to think.

"How did you know who I was?"

"The lady next door gave me your license plate number," Ravon said.

"I saw something on the news about the police charging your sister with something."

"Yeah, that's what she said. She has an attorney so she should be okay. She couldn't hurt a fly."

Ian nodded his head.

"Is there anything that you can tell me? I'm afraid the police are going to try to pin this on me."

"Why would they do that?"

"Because I'm an easy target."

"I see," Ian said. "Well, the only thing I did was drop her off. Some clown was chasing her out into the street and I almost hit her."

"She said she gave you a key."

"She did," Ian said, nodding his head. "I took the key, went into her place. The man was still assaulting her and I put a stop to that. She was in pretty bad shape but she gave me her mother's address. I took her there and that's the last time I saw her. I wish I could help you more. She's been on my mind. I hate cowards and that man she was with is certainly one of them."

Ravon sighed. His nerves were getting worse and he looked around nervously.

"Are you okay?"

"Yeah," Ravon said. "Well, I'm sorry to bother you."

"You're okay. You're not bothering me at all."

Ian looked up to see a motorcycle racing down his street. Two people, both wearing black, were riding on one bike. They caught his attention because the one on the back was facing the rear of the bike. That was strange. "Oh shit."

POW. POW. POW. POW. POW. POW. POW. An automatic weapon let off a slew of shots directly at him.

Ian jumped back behind his door and hit the floor. Once the shooting had ceased, he stuck his arm out of the door and grabbed Ravon's leg, pulling him into the house.

Ian looked back to make sure KJ was okay and noticed the boy still sitting at the table with his fork stopped midway to his mouth.

"Get down, boy," Ian snapped. Once KJ was safely on the floor, he turned his attention back to Ravon.

"Are you hit?"

"No," Ravon said. "I'm good."

Ian jumped up and ran to his bedroom to retrieve his own gun. He chambered a round and walked back out to the living room.

"Call nine-one-one," he said to KJ, then turned to Ravon. "And you come with me."

They walked out onto the porch and Ian looked down the street where the motorcycle had gone but didn't see anything.

"What kind of foolishness are you bringing to me, boy?"

"Nobody knows I'm over here. Maybe they're after you," Ravon said.

Ian ignored him and continued to walk down his street toward where the bike had gone. As he walked, he thought he noticed something in the middle of the street. He strained his eyes and realized that it was the bike lying on its side. Both of the men picked up their pace until they reached the carnage. Willie and Harry were standing by two men wearing black leather riding suits. The bike was a little further down and beside it was a bloody sword. One of the men was lying in the street with a deep laceration across his chest. Blood was pouring from his cut and he was lying on his back, grimacing in pain. The other rider was sitting up with his hands behind his head as if he was about to be arrested by Harry, who had a gun trained on him. One of the men was white and the other one was black.

"Good Lord," Ian said as he watched the man's blood rush from his body.

"Didn't I tell you we take care of this block?" Willie said to Ravon. "These yo' friends?"

"No," Ravon said as he studied the face of the white man. "I don't know who they are."

"Who the hell ya'll shooting at?" Willie asked the unresponsive white guy with the ponytail.

Ian walked over to Ponytail and kneeled down. "What's the problem?" he whispered.

"Just doing my job," Ponytail said.

"What job is that?" Ian asked.

"Is your name Ian DeMarco?"

"Yep."

"My job is to take you out. You should mind your own business," the white guy said as cool as the other side of the pillow.

"Who wants me dead?"

"It's not important," the man said with a smirk. "I'll never tell."

"Oh, yes the hell you will," Willie said as he walked over and picked up his sword. "Or I will chop your muthafucking head off."

Ponytail looked up as if the thought of death brought no fear to him.

Willie lifted the sword over his head. "You got to the count of three, damn it. One...Two...."

"Do it," the man said with a straight face.

Two police cars came rushing down the street toward them, forcing Willie to put down his weapon. He nodded his head toward Harry and they casually walked away from the crime scene.

Z ola sat up and placed her hand on the area of her chest where the business end of the taser had hit her. Surprisingly, she didn't feel any residual pain. She quickly made it to her feet and rushed to her bedroom to get dressed. Her mind raced as she threw on a pair of workout tights, a hooded sweatshirt and a pair of Nike running shoes. Her cell phone rang and she looked at the caller ID. It was Kecia.

"They took Jason," she said calmly into the phone. "Will you call the attorney and tell her that for me? I'm going to get my son."

"I'm at my desk and I thought I saw the police leaving out of the side door. Oh, my God."

"Yeah. I'm leaving now. Will you make that call for me?"

"I will call her now. Where are you going?"

"Out to the Benjamins. They are not keeping my son. I never gave them custody. I don't know what kind of lie that bitch told these assholes who came in here," Zola said as she grabbed her car keys from the hook on the kitchen wall. "But I refuse to allow her to try to poison my son's mind with her foolishness."

"I'll call Sharon right now, but please don't do anything that will get you in trouble, Zola."

"I'll be fine. I need to go."

Zola pressed the end key on the phone without waiting on a response. She stopped in her tracks, thought for a second, and then walked back to her bedroom and lifted her mattress. She grabbed the silver .32 automatic handgun and tossed it in her purse. There was no limit on how far she was willing to go in order to bring her child home.

Zola raced from her condo, ran down the hallway, and hit the emergency exit. She took the stairs three steps at a time. Kecia was waiting on her when she reached the lobby.

"I spoke with Sharon and she told me to tell you not to go out there," Kecia said.

Zola walked past her without a word.

"Zola," Kecia said. "Please don't go out there. Let Sharon handle this."

Zola pushed through the glass door and rushed out into the parking lot, bumping into an old white couple and knocking their groceries onto the ground. She didn't bother to apologize as she ran and jumped into her Jaguar. She started the engine and sped out of the parking garage onto Moreland Avenue without looking. A car slammed on its brakes and barely missed her. The driver screamed profanities at her, but Zola was in a zone.

The weekends were always great for driving as the majority of working people who clogged the expressways were enjoying a few days of relaxation. Highway I-20 was clear as freshly cleaned glass. Zola pressed down on the gas pedal in her high-powered sports car and was doing over one hundred miles per hour in a matter of seconds. She had tunnel vision and was completely focused on getting her son back. She made it to I-85 North and slowed down when she noticed two Georgia State Troopers parked on the side of the road. Once she passed them, she jumped onto I-285 West to GA-400. She took the familiar north ramp out to Alpharetta where the Benjamins lived. She looked into her rearview mirror and saw a police car coming up. She eased off of the gas pedal and looked down at her speedometer;

she was doing seventy miles per hour. Zola moved over into the far right lane but the car sped past her. She kept her speed steady for the next two exits and got off on the Old Milton Parkway exit. A few more twists and turns and she was at the gate of the exclusive Country Club North subdivision. Finally catching a break, the gate was wide open and the security guard wasn't at the guard's quarters. Zola sped through and headed straight toward the Benjamins' opulent estate, which sat on five acres of highly manicured Bermuda grass.

Much to her surprise, police cars were everywhere. Seeing this made her even more nervous. Zola pulled into the driveway and jumped out of the car. As she was running up to the house, she saw a handcuffed Carmen Benjamin being led off by a police officer.

"Where is my son?!" she screamed at the redheaded lady who looked like she hadn't slept in days.

Carmen stopped and stared at Zola.

"Where is my son?" Zola asked again.

"Don't you dare use that tone with me, you unfit piece of ghetto trash," the woman said. "Do you know who you're talking to? I gave him everything and all you could give him was some roach-infested projects. You'll never get him back."

Zola ran after the woman; a police officer tried to grab her, but she slipped past him and made it to Carmen. Zola reared back, punched the white woman in the head, then swung again, catching Carmen in the back of the head as she went down. The policemen who were holding her saved her from smacking her face on the driveway. A skinny rookie officer, who looked like Carrot Top, ran over and restrained Zola. He threw her to the ground, placed his knee in the small of her back and handcuffed her.

"Let her go," a voice said.

Zola turned her head and looked into the face of Detective Shilo.

"Sir," the officer pleaded. "I just witnessed her assault that woman."

"I said, let her go," the detective said in a stern voice that Zola had never heard him use.

Officer Carrot Top shook his head but did as he was told.

"Help her up," Detective Shilo said to the officer. "And apologize."

The officer frowned at him but gave a half-hearted apology.

Detective Shilo walked over to Zola. "Are you okay??"

"Where is Jason?"

"He's fine. We have him down at the station. We're trying to locate the judge so that he can lift the order and get him back where he needs to be."

Zola's eyes lit up. "For good?"

"That's up to the judge, but I have a feeling that once he sees what's going on here, he won't have too much of a choice."

"What's going on here?"

"Your friend, Andy, aka Andre, spilled the beans. He was working for the Benjamins. Their plan was for him to woo you until you trusted him enough to commit a crime for him. Once that crime was committed, you were going to get caught and be sent to prison. Once you were in jail, they would have Jason all to themselves.

"What they didn't count on was him starting to develop real feelings for you. He wanted out but they had come too far, so they…"

"Wait a minute. Did you just say, 'they'?"

"Yes," Detective Shilo said, nodding his bald head. "Mr. Benjamin was in on it, too. They offered to pay Mr. Dubois one million dollars for you to disappear. Didn't matter if he killed you or had you killed, but like I said, he really liked you and just couldn't bring himself to do it. So they tried to have him killed."

Zola was shocked and appalled all at the same time.

"When can I get my son?"

"I'm not sure. You should have your attorney look into that for you."

Just then, a white Range Rover pulled up in front of the house. Mr. Benjamin got out looking as if he was about to roll some heads, but before he could open his mouth, he was rushed by three police officers. He placed his hands in the air and surrendered peacefully.

Chad Benjamin made eye contact with Zola and she gave him a look that could kill an elephant. Chad dropped his head and walked with the police to a waiting car.

"Thank you for everything, Detective," Zola said.

"Don't mention it," Detective Shilo said. "Just doing my job."

"Mrs. Zaire," Detective Sullivan, Shilo's thin and nasty partner, walked up looking at his trusty notepad. "I have some bad news."

"You're bad news," Zola said.

"This case is deeper than meets the eye. These are not some people who happened to fall in love with your son and went overboard."

"Get to the point," Zola snapped.

The detective looked down at his notepad and frowned. "Your mother, Ms. Sara Zaire, set this whole thing up from start to finish."

"What do you mean, she set this whole thing up?" Zola said, feeling anger rise to the surface.

"She set it up. She used to work for the Benjamins. When the state got involved with taking your son, she asked the Benjamins to step in. They did, but they didn't want to give up custody. She started putting a little pressure on them, and like I said, she worked for them so she knew a few of their secrets. Well, anyway, she threatened to blow the lid off of some other information that would bring their little world crashing down and the Benjamins decided to have her taken out. I'm a little concerned right now because there is another target out there. I want to know if you can help me save this man's life."

"What man?" Zola asked, still trying to digest the news that had just rocked her world.

"Who is Ian DeMarco?"

"I don't know that name," she said.

"Ms. Zaire," Detective Sullivan said. "Stay with me now. Time is precious. We're trying to save a life."

"I told you, I never heard that name," she said, raising her voice.

"Are you telling me the truth or are you following some street code?"

"For the third time, I don't know that damn name!"

"My research tells me that you do know him and like I said, I have reason to believe that his life is in danger as well," Detective Sullivan said.

"Well, your research is faulty," Zola countered.

Detective Sullivan shook his head and walked off without another word.

Zola sighed and looked up at the huge white mansion. She shook her head at all of that wealth and could only wish she had a fraction of it, but then she hunched her shoulders as she realized that even with all of their wealth, both Benjamins were sitting in the back of police cars as if they were common criminals.

She turned and reached out her hand toward Detective Shilo. "Thank you so much."

"Good luck, Ms. Zaire," he said as he walked beside her toward her car.

"When is the last time you spoke with your brother?" he asked.

Zola stopped walking and turned to face the man. "Why?"

"I have reason to believe that he may be the one who killed the man who killed your mother."

"No," she said as she felt her legs get weak. The last thing she wanted to see was her brother shipped back off to prison.

"Nobody knows but me, and my source and I are thinking about keeping it that way. It was pretty obvious to me that it was a justifiable homicide, but given his history, I'm not so sure a jury would see it that way. So I think I'm going to keep my findings to myself."

Zola looked at the man and wanted to hug his fat neck, but instead she placed both of her hands on one of his and gave it a tight squeeze. "Thank you."

"Don't mention it," Detective Shilo said. "I'm serious. Don't mention it. Not even to him."

"You have my word on it."

Detective Shilo handed her a business card. "I'd like for you to call me if you have any problems, Ms. Zaire. I'd like to consider myself one of the good guys."

Zola smiled and nodded her head. "It's good to know that we still have good guys on the police force."

"I grew up poor and I know firsthand how we were treated, so I made it my business to change the system from within."

"That's good to know," she said before opening her car door and sitting inside. "And I'll be sure to keep your card."

"Please do. Take care and keep me posted on your son. I have a feeling everything will work out fine."

"From your mouth to God's ears," she said before backing out of the driveway.

26

"Thanks for your help, man," Ravon said as he reached out to shake Ian's hand. "I appreciate you looking out for my sister, too."

"No problem," Ian said. "Will you give me her phone number? I'd like to check up on her."

"I'm sure she won't mind," Ravon said as he spit out the numbers that Ian recorded into his cell phone.

"I need to get out of here," Ravon said.

"Me, too," Ian said as they walked back toward his house. "I'm going house hunting today. "I've had enough of this ghetto living."

"You gonna sell your house?"

"Yep," Ian said. "You wanna buy it?"

"Man," Ravon said. "I wish I could buy a candy bar. I have a feeling I'm going to be spending any money I make on a lawyer."

"Why is that?"

Ravon gave Ian a quick rundown of the events that had taken place over the last few days and once he was done, Ian shook his head. He knew all too well what the young man was going through.

"I have a very good attorney," he said. "I can have him take your call."

"The problem is, my pockets can only afford a public defender and you know what that will get you."

"Twenty-five to life," Ian said.

"Correct."

"Don't worry about the money. Are you working?"

"No," Ravon said.

"Do you want a job?"

"Yeah," he said.

"Take my number down and give me a call on Monday," Ian said. "As long as you don't mind riding a trash truck, I may be able to help you."

"Man," Ravon said, "I'll ride in the trash."

The two men shared a laugh and a handshake before Ravon got into his car and pulled off.

Ian turned and walked into his yard just as an ambulance was pulling up. He paused on his front porch and motioned toward the driver that their help was needed down the street. The passenger nodded at him and pulled off.

"Uncle Ian," KJ said, still shaken from all of the gunshots. "Look!"

KJ was pointing at a bullet hole that was in the wall of Christian's room. It went straight through his pillow.

"Oh my God," he said as his knees threatened to give out on him.

Ian sat on the bed and took a moment. He had lost his entire world due to violence and here it was again. All he could think of was his son getting killed in his sleep.

His thoughts were broken up when he looked out of the window and saw something on the ground. He turned on his heels and raced from the house. He jumped off of the front porch and ran to the side of his house where he saw Trudy lying on the ground. She was lying flat on her back and gasping for air. She was losing the battle to stay alive. He noticed the front of her dirty shirt was red with blood. A bullet had caught her in the chest and she was barely hanging on. Ian stood and ran out to the street to see if the paramedics were still down there working on the shooters. They were. He yelled out to them and one of them came running.

"My friend is shot back here," he said as he led the man to where Trudy was. A few tears welled up in his eyes. "Do you think she's gonna make it?"

"Don't know," the guy said as he immediately fell to his knees and started tending to her.

The paramedic said something into his radio and the ambulance backed up. The driver got out and opened the back door.

"Will you help me get her to the truck?" the paramedic asked Ian.

"Sure," Ian said as they lifted the battered and bruised woman up and carried her to the waiting vehicle.

Ian looked up to see Willie and Harry walking through the path leading to his house. For the first time since he had known him, Willie didn't have his sword. The old man looked at Trudy and burst out crying. His legs gave way and Harry had to hold him up.

Ian shook his head as they closed the door to take his friend away.

"Are they going to take her to Grady?" Ian asked a police officer who walked up.

"Yes. What's her name?"

"Trudy Blackwell. She used to be a doctor."

The police officer shook his head. "Are you serious? A real doctor?"

"Yeah," Ian said.

"That's such a shame," the officer said.

"Yeah," Ian said. "I want those guys charged to the fullest extent of the law. A bullet hit my son's bed. Thank God that he is with my sister. But I want them charged with attempted murder."

The officer nodded his head. "May I see what you're talking about?"

"Yep," Ian said as he led the man into his house.

Once the officer had all of the information he needed, Ian walked with him back outside and said goodbye. He stayed on the front porch. Willie and Harry were sitting on the rocking chairs. Ian walked over and took a seat beside them. The three men sat lost in their own worlds as they watched the chaos that was unfolding around them. Police cars, ambulances, a chopped up body, bullet holes, and near-death experiences were all a part of life in the hood.

"Fellas," Ian said. "I'm moving. Once I get settled into my new place, I will have you guys over for dinner."

Neither of the men acknowledged Ian's invitation. They were too lost in the moment.

Ian stood and walked back into his house.

"KJ," he said. "I want you to go into Christian's room and gather up as many of his clothes as you can. We won't be coming back here."

Once they had every one of his son's belongings loaded into his truck, Ian walked back into the house and grabbed a few of his personal items and tossed them into a bag. Everything else could stay.

"Go ahead and get in the car, KJ," Ian said to his nephew.

He walked over to Willie and Harry.

"Fellas," he said, "I'm moving on."

Neither of the men responded.

He reached out and handed Willie the key to his house. "Here you go," he said. "I need a favor. Once Trudy gets better, I want you to give her this key. You tell her I will be back over here to check on her from time to time, but this house is hers."

"You a good man, Ian. A damn good man," Harry said, nodding his head vigorously.

"One of the best to ever put on a pair of pants," Willie echoed, but stared straight ahead.

"Y'all not bad either," Ian said as he turned and walked away. "God bless ya both."

"We gonna need it," Harry said. "We sho' gonna need it, living round here. God bless us all."

EPILOGUE

"Happy birthday to you. Happy Birthday to you. Happy Birthday, dear Jason. Happy Birthday to you," the crowd of ten adults and twenty kids sang.

Zola was all smiles as she looked around the house at all of her new and old friends. The doorbell rang and Detective Shilo and his wife were standing on the other side. He handed her a large, brightly wrapped box for Jason.

"I'm so happy you could make it," she said to the man who had been nothing short of a blessing to her and her family. It had been six months since the police officers came and took her son away. It took another week for her to get Jason back with her full-time, but since that moment, they had been one happy family. Ravon's role in the white man's murder was never mentioned and for that, Detective Shilo had cemented himself as a true friend in her heart.

"It's been a long time, Zola. And let me tell you, you look absolutely gorgeous," he said. "This is my wife, Thelma."

"It's nice to meet you, Thelma," Zola said, reaching out to hug the woman whose husband she credited with saving her life. Zola always gave Detective Shilo that credit because without him, she would be sitting in a jail cell right now. It was his thorough detective work that put the right people behind bars. Shortly after their arrest, the walls came tumbling down on the Benjamins. The courts canceled Zola's temporary custody release and placed

Jason back in her care full-time. Andre/Andy was sitting in a prison cell and would be there for a very long time for his role in the Benjamins' scheme.

"You guys make yourselves at home," Zola said. "There is plenty of food and punch."

"Thank you. But let me tell you," Shilo said, "your son is going to be an attorney. He's so smart. Without him, I'm not sure we would've gotten a conviction."

"Thank you," Zola said.

"Feel good," the detective said. "No need to hold him back."

"Do you need anything else?" Ian said as he walked up to Zola.

"Look who's here," Zola said.

"Hey, man," Ian said to the man whom he had heard so much about. "The guys are all downstairs. The Falcons' game is about to come on."

"With all of this company in here, Ian?" Zola said with a frown.

"I'm all yours Monday through Friday, baby, but the weekend belongs to me. It's the playoffs. What more can I say? Eagles and Falcons," Ian said, looking at his watch. "Kick off in six minutes."

"Let him go, girl," Thelma said. "Trying to get between a man and his football is a losing battle."

"Yeah," Ian said, nodding his head. "Listen to her. I already gave away my tickets to the game and now I'm not about to miss it on television."

"Man," Willie said, walking into the kitchen area. He was cleaned up nicely but refused to take his sword off his hip. "I need something a little stronger than punch."

"Hey, Willie," Harry said, motioning him over. "I found the stash. Come on."

Ian smiled and shook his head.

"Oh, Lord," Zola said. "You and your friends."

"Speaking of friends, look what the cat done drug in," he said, looking at Walker and all of his kids coming through the front door.

"Damn, Walker. What did you do, rent a school bus?" Ian said as he walked over and shook his friend's hand. He reached out and gave his wife a hug.

"Yes," Walker said. "I knew you was rich. Look at dis house, man? You holding out, brodda. Give me a job where you working."

"We'll talk about it," Ian said. "All of the guys are downstairs and that's where I'm headed, too."

"You're leaving up here for real, hunh?" Zola said.

Ian leaned over and gave her a kiss on her lips. They had been an item since his phone call to her on the day he moved out of his house in the West End. A few dates to the movies and dinner was all he needed to know that she was the one for him.

"Four minutes until kickoff," Ian said with a smile. "Come on, Shilo."

"I'm going to remember this," Zola said, pretending to be upset.

Ian shook his head as if he wasn't falling for that one and made his way downstairs to their full basement. "I'll send your brother up here to help you."

Ravon was sitting on the sofa, yelling at the television because the Eagles ran the opening kickoff back for a touchdown.

"Come on, Ray," KJ said with a smile. "Don't hate."

"KJ," Ravon said. "How can you be an Eagles fan when you're born and raised right here in Atlanta?"

"Mike Vick," he said as if that was all that needed to be said.

"Whatever," Ravon said while still frowning. "I like Vick, too, but he's with the enemy now so forget him."

"Nah," KJ said. "Forget the Falcons. Those hypocrites had the nerve to get mad because the man fought some dogs. I bet the owner went deer hunting the same day they released him. At least the dogs had a fair chance against another dog. The deer ain't gonna win against a high-powered rifle."

"What's up, Pops?" Ian said as he plopped down in a chair beside his dad. "Are you okay?"

Colin DeMarco smiled. Christian was on the floor by his feet, playing with his cars, and the old man looked like he had died and gone to heaven.

"I'm doing just fine," he said. "I love this house, boy."

"Thank you."

"And you have a very good woman upstairs. Nobody will ever replace Tasha, but God is good. That woman and her son are heaven sent; please believe that."

"I do," Ian said.

"And you're back with the family business, which is the only reason I worked so hard all of those years. I never wanted my kids to ever have to beg anybody for a job. Malcolm is handling the west coast expansion and I couldn't be happier."

"Malcolm just called."

"I heard him and Andrea on the phone arguing," Colin said. "Those two want to be buried next to each other so they can fuss in the afterlife."

"Probably," Ian said with a smile.

"I want a beer," Colin said, and before he could finish his sentence, Willie handed him one from the stash he had in his cargo pockets.

"You're not supposed to steal from folks when they invite you into their home, idiot," Harry said.

"I'm not stealing. I was saving myself a trip to the fridge, stupid."

"Who you calling stupid, you ugly…"

"Oh, Lord. You guys aren't happy unless y'all are going at each other," Ian said as he noticed Jason staring at him. He stood and walked over to where the little boy was sitting all alone in a corner.

"What's up, Jason? You don't like football?"

"No," he said with a smile. "I'm really not into any sports. I played soccer last year, but I didn't like that either."

"Are you enjoying your party?"

"Yes," he said, nodding his head. "Thanks."

"No need to thank me. It's your birthday."

Jason nodded his head.

"What's on your mind?"

"Do you like my mom?"

"I do. I like her a lot. I like you, too. Do you like me?"

Jason hunched his shoulders. "I'm not sure."

Ian frowned.

"My mom has been through a lot, Mr. Ian. My dad was an older guy who took advantage of her. She's young, but she's been through more than most fifty-year-old women."

"I know, but we are looking forward not back."

"I read lots of stuff about her when I was living with the Benjamins, stuff I probably shouldn't have read, but I did. Did you know that she had never been with a man because she loved him?"

"We've talked about that."

"She seems happy with you. You're the first person she's ever *wanted* to be with. Everyone else, she felt like she had to be with them for whatever reason."

"Well, I'm very happy to hear that she wants to be with me. I want to be with her, too."

"She doesn't need a boyfriend who will break her heart in a few months. She needs to stay happy forever."

"I'll try my best."

"Do you know what I realized?"

"What's that, Jason?" Ian asked.

"My mom's the best mom in the world. She let me go live with some strangers because she loves me more than she loves herself. She's the prettiest woman in the world, too. I don't care what I read in those papers about her past. She's perfect. God made her that way."

"I agree."

"To me, she's pure as they come."

"You won't get an argument out of me on that one, buddy."

"You know what else, Mr. Ian?"

"What's that?"

"Being that she's never given herself to a man, my momma's a virgin."

Ian smiled and rubbed Jason's head. "You are one deep young man. Now go upstairs and enjoy your party."

ABOUT THE AUTHOR

Travis Hunter is an author, songwriter and screenwriter. A veteran of the U.S. Army, he lives in Atlanta and is the founder of the Hearts of Men Foundation, a program that mentors underprivileged children. Visit www.travishunter.com.